P9-CLO-859

"You want me to see your dad."

"And," Kyle continued, "you want me to pay for him to have his operation privately?"

"Yes," Heather agreed baldly. "But not because I think you owe them anything, Kyle. If you want to think of it as a payment, then tell yourself it's payment to me for finally admitting what I've really known for years. That my parents love and need you...possibly more than they love and need me."

There, she'd said it. She couldn't endure any more. She turned and headed blindly for the door.

"Heather." She winced as his fingers caught her shoulder. "What's wrong?"

"I didn't come here to discuss my private life, Kyle."

"As I understand it, there isn't much to talk about."

Heather frowned. How could Kyle know anything about her personal life?

PENNY JORDAN was constantly in trouble in school because of her inability to stop daydreaming—especially during French lessons. In her teens she was an avid romance reader, although it didn't occur to her to try writing one herself until she was older. "My first half-dozen attempts ended up ingloriously," she remembers, "but I persevered, and one manuscript was finished." She plucked up the courage to send it to a publisher, convinced her book would be rejected. It wasn't, and the rest is history! Penny is married and lives in Cheshire.

Books by Penny Jordan

Don't miss any of our special offers. Write to us at the following address for information on our newest releases.

Harlequin Reader Service
901 Fuhrmann Blvd., P.O. Box 1397, Buffalo, NY 14240
Canadian address: P.O. Box 603,
Fort Erie, Ont. L2A 5X3

PENNY JORDAN

payment in love

Harlequin Books

TORONTO • NEW YORK • LONDON
AMSTERDAM • PARIS • SYDNEY • HAMBURG
STOCKHOLM • ATHENS • TOKYO • MILAN

Harlequin Presents first edition November 1990
ISBN 0-373-11314-5

Original hardcover edition published in 1988
by Mills & Boon Limited

Copyright © 1988 by Penny Jordan. All rights reserved.
Except for use in any review, the reproduction or utilization
of this work in whole or in part in any form by any electronic,
mechanical or other means, now known or hereafter invented,
including xerography, photocopying and recording,
or in any information storage or retrieval system, is forbidden without
the permission of the publisher, Harlequin Enterprises Limited,
225 Duncan Mill Road, Don Mills, Ontario, Canada M3B 3K9.

All the characters in this book have no existence outside the
imagination of the author and have no relation whatsoever to
anyone bearing the same name or names. They are not even
distantly inspired by any individual known or unknown to the
author, and all incidents are pure invention.

® are Trademarks registered in the United States Patent and
Trademark Office and in other countries.

Printed in U.S.A.

CHAPTER ONE

THE sitting room was strewn with pieces of dissected fir tree, and the reel of scarlet tartan ribbon the cat had unrolled made bright pools of colour against the dark background of the carpet. Heather noticed these details as she walked into the room, just as she saw how the flickering flames from the apple logs in the fireplace threw cheerful shadows to lighten the dreariness of the darkening winter's afternoon. She couldn't help noticing them—that was how she had been brought up, to observe and then store what she had seen for use later on—but today she noticed them absently, without her normal enthusiasm.

She had just finished speaking to her mother, and what she had heard had not reassured her. It was hard to believe that it was less than two days since her father had been rushed into hospital.

Neither she nor her mother had known there was anything wrong. Gordon Burns was a lean, tanned man in his late fifties, with a boundless energy for life that nothing seemed to quench.

Even now, when his shock of once dark hair had turned iron-grey, Heather still had difficulty in accepting the fact that he was growing older. She frowned and nibbled tensely at her bottom lip. They had always been such a closely knit family.

Many of her contemporaries found it odd that she should not only be quite content working for her parents, but that she should also voluntarily choose to live at home. At twenty-three, she supposed she *was* rather unusual, but she had never felt any desire to share their so-called independence.

The phone rang sharply and she hurried to answer it, her heart racing. It could be her mother again from the hospital. They had agreed she would ring only when there was anything to report. So far, her father's condition was stable, although there was talk of the necessity of an operation to bypass some of the damaged arteries, and avert the danger of further heart attacks.

Only last night the specialist had cautioned them about the seriousness of her father's condition. Such an operation would have to be carried out privately, Heather knew, and again she gnawed distractedly on her bottom lip. A tall, slender girl, she took after her father more than her petite blond-haired mother; she had his colouring and his dark red hair, but in temperament she was like neither of her parents. A throwback to the MacDonald clan, with its reputation for fierce pride and intense emotions, so her father often teased her, and it was true. As a child and a teenager, the intensity of her own bewildering emotions had often left her disturbed and defensive. Now, as an adult, she had learned, if not to control them, then at least to understand them.

She picked up the receiver, her mouth dry with apprehension, but it was only Mrs Anstey, the mainstay of their small village population and the uncrowned head of the local Women's Institute.

'Heather, my dear, I'm sorry to bother you at a time like this, but how are you doing with the decorations?'

Many years ago, Heather's father had worked in London's top store as a departmental manager, and it was while he was there that he had conceived the idea of starting up his own business to make and supply to small shops the kind of window-dressing and design service normally only available to stores large and profitable enough to afford an in-house window-dressing team.

In retrospect, even Gordon Burns had been surprised by the success of his small venture. Within two years of starting up in business, his wife had joined the company, and then, once she left art school, Heather had been co-opted on to the team.

Normally, she loved her work. There was something immensely satisfying about being given a relatively small budget and then asked to create the impossible.

Over the years her father had been approached several times with offers to buy him out, but he had insisted that he liked his business the way it was, small and modestly successful.

If her father had one fault, it was that he was too soft-hearted; too generous, Heather acknowledged wryly; and the Christmas party for the old folk's home was a prime example of his generosity.

When Maureen Anstey had approached him about decorating the church hall for the party, he had immediately thrown himself into the preparations with vigour and enthusiasm, and Heather knew from past experience that, when it came to submitting his invoice, the sum quoted would have very little bearing on the actual cost of time and materials.

They had always had a comfortable life-style, but she knew that her parents had no savings, nothing to finance something as expensive as the open-heart surgery it now seemed her father was going to need.

She had been the one to find him, slumped over his desk in his study, and the shock of that discovery was still with her, adding a new vulnerability to her shadowed eyes and full mouth.

Having assured Maureen Anstey that the decorations would be completed in time, she returned to the sitting-room. For once, the sight of it failed to soothe her. The sitting-room was her favourite room in the small rectory her parents had bought when they first moved down to Durminster. All the downstairs rooms had open fires, and this room, with its collection of comfortably old furniture and its general air of being very much a family room, had an immediate ambience of warmth.

The cat miaowed plaintively, reminding her that it was tea time. She would have to take Meg out for a walk before it got too dark.

The old collie thumped her tail on the kitchen floor as Heather walked in. Meg had been a thirteenth birthday present to her. A shiver suddenly touched her skin, as memories she would rather not have had slid, betraying, to the surface of her mind. How clearly she could picture that birthday morning. Her parents' faces, happy and expectant, the excited yaps of the small puppy; it should have been the most perfect of memories, but it was marred by another face, sharp and haunting still, after all these years.

As she had reached out to take hold of the puppy, her mother had said warmly, 'Of course, you must share Meg with Kyle, Heather.'

And instantly she had dropped the little pup back into her box. Even now, down the years, she could still hear the truculent bitterness in her childish voice as she'd said bitterly, 'I don't want her, then. You can give her to him, because I'm not sharing her.'

Even now, the memory had the power to make her suffer a wild see-saw of emotions, some of them so complex and still so only partially understood by herself that she could scarcely bear their oppressiveness.

She had been jealous, of course. Bitterly and immensely jealous, and the remnant of that jealousy and what it had led her to do still haunted her.

One of her closest friends at art school had accused her of being motivated by guilt when Heather had explained to her why she felt she must go home and work with her parents, and she had been partially right. Deep in her heart, she knew that nothing she could ever do could wipe out what she had once done; there was no going back and, even though her actions had been those of an immature child, their repercussions still echoed through all their lives.

She had been seven when her parents first mooted the idea of fostering a teenage boy. She had hated the idea right from the start, resentful of their need to introduce someone else into their small family circle, but she might have grown to accept the idea if she had not happened to overhear someone commenting that they suspected that her mother had never really got over the loss of the baby boy she had been carrying before Heather's own birth.

Until that moment, she had never known that she might have had an elder brother, and with that knowledge had come the first seeds of doubt about the strength of her parents' love for her.

While they talked about their fortunate circumstances and the value of sharing them with someone less fortunate, she had grown more and more bitterly resentful of the as yet unknown male intruder who was apparently more important to her parents' lives then she was herself.

And her resentment and fear had grown, so much so that, well before the social worker had brought Kyle to see them, she had already hated him.

She had steadfastly refused to go with her parents on their visits to the children's home, bitterly resentful of their determination to carry out their plans in the face of her own strongly voiced and expressed disapproval.

She knew now that her disapproval had only increased her father's determination, and that he had been disturbed by her displays of temper and jealousy, for her own sake. At the time, she had simply seen, in their calm continuation with their plans, a total lack of regard for her and her feelings, which had increased her fear that she wasn't loved or wanted and that this stranger would supplant her in her parents' lives.

They had known none of this, simply seeing in her resentment and anger an only child's lack of vision and narrowed upbringing. Both of them had been only children themselves, and were far more aware of the pitfalls that could lurk ahead than

Heather herself, but she had not known of any of this.

The seeds of resentment and hatred had been sown, and when Kyle had finally arrived she'd been determined to hate him.

And hate him she had. It hadn't been hard. For one thing, he was obviously bigger and more powerful than she was, a whole six years older, and thirteen to her seven; for another, he was a whole lot cleverer as well, talking with her parents on a level that totally excluded her.

Now, of course, she could see that Kyle had felt just as insecure as she had herself, that the fact that he had totally ignored her had sprung from feelings very close to those she was herself experiencing, and not a desire to cut her out of her parents' love.

She also knew now that love was something that wasn't necessarily apportioned; and that it was something that grew rather than diminished when it was shared with others. Yes, she knew all these things now. Now, when it was too late.

She frowned and reached for her hooded duffel coat. It was cold outside. Snow threatened; she could smell it in the air.

Meg barked excitedly as she opened the door. At the back of the rectory garden was a stile and a footpath that led through the fields. It had been a clear, bright day, and as she climbed over the stile the fields lay spread out against a winter skyline, the sky that deep, dense dark blue that only occurred on very cold and clear winter evenings. The full moon illuminated the scene brilliantly, and her breath hung on the air in steamy puffballs of vapour. The sharpness of Meg's yaps was intensified by the crystal clearness of the air, and far away a farm dog heard it and set up a bark in response.

From the copse Heather heard the unearthly cry of a dog fox, and Meg pricked up her ears. Some instincts never died, Heather acknowledged, shaking her head at the collie as she crouched, belly down, on the crisp frosted field.

It was just the right sort of evening for a brisk walk, the sort of evening she would normally have thoroughly enjoyed. She knew that her parents sometimes worried about her solitary state; her mother was constantly urging her to join in the village's extremely varied social gatherings, but so far she had not experienced any desire to find a mate and settle down, and she knew herself well enough to accept that a string of casual relationships was not for her.

She was frightened of committing herself in a male-to-female relationship, she knew that. Her experiences of the intensity and depth of her capability for emotion had affected her in the same way a small child reacts to an accidental burn when faced with the threat of a real fire: she shied away, apprehensive and alarmed, remembering past pain.

The relationship between her parents, its stability and longevity, had spoiled her; she could not adopt the careless manner of her contemporaries towards the commitment of marriage, and she doubted that she would ever find a man who could and would commit himself to her with the wholeheartedness she knew that she would crave if she ever allowed herself to fall in love.

That being the case, she was better off not allowing herself to do so. The heady sixties with its *laissez-faire* attitude towards casual sex had gone, and in its place was a new awareness, a new carefulness about the use and abuse of the human body. One was no longer considered odd if one did not agree to go to bed with a man on a first date, and Heather preferred things that way.

She did date occasionally—boys, now adult, whom she'd known from school, men she met through her work—but so far there had been no one special in her life; no lover.

Frost crunched underfoot as she took the familiar path. Meg darted off to investigate a long empty rabbit burrow. This route was well known to both of them, and yet she always found something new about it, Heather acknowledged, her heavy thoughts dismissed momentarily as her artist's eye was caught by the black and silver tracery of bare branches illuminated by the moon.

The weather men were predicting snow for Christmas. Maureen Anstey had commented wryly that the village children were delighted. Not so pleased were those members of the community whose jobs meant driving daily to Bath and Bristol. This part of the country was notorious for its heavy winter snowfalls, and the opening of the M4 had suddenly made it far more accessible to London-based businessmen looking for a country environment for their wives and families. A small influx of newcomers during the summer months had added to the population, but Heather wondered how many of them realised what they would have to face during the winter months.

Their coal-house was already stacked with fuel, the logs her father had cut only two weekends ago drying out; gas had been bought in ready for their annual power-cuts. She remembered how astonished Kyle had been by the depth of their snowfalls. He had come from London, where snow never lay for very long on the busy streets. Just momentarily she had felt superior to him but, as always, he had quickly turned the tables on her. She shivered and called to Meg.

She knew why Kyle Bennett was in her thoughts so much, of course; she had known from the first moment the specialist had told them that her father was going to need surgery and she had seen the fear and exhaustion on her mother's face.

Things had not been going well for them businesswise recently. Too many shops were closing; too many small businesses going to the wall. It hadn't helped, seeing all those huge signs plastered all over Bristol for Bennett Enterprises. Who would ever have thought that the scruffy-at-heel boy her parents had taken in would turn out to be such a successful businessman?

He was a millionaire several times over now, and with a life-style to match his wealth, if the popular Press was to be believed. And, knowing him as she did, Heather did believe it.

He had always liked the very best life had to offer, she remembered sourly. She only had to think of the succession of pouting would-be model girls he had brought home to show off to her parents. Glossy, expensive creatures who had made her feel clumsy and ugly, and she had seen in his eyes that he had known and enjoyed her discomfort.

It had always been like that between them. From the very first moment, they had recognised in each other a mortal enemy. She had never imagined then that *she* would be the one to vanquish *him*. She shivered, and not from the cold, remembering the price that had had to be paid for her victory. And she had not been the one to pay it. She swallowed hard against the lump of pain buried deep in her throat. Her parents never mentioned him, never referred to the events of that dreadful night, the night of her seventeenth birthday. They had never reproached or condemned, but she knew how they must feel. In demonstrating the strength of their love for her, they had also shown her a mirror-image of her own selfishness, an image reinforced by the counselling she had received while in hospital. She shuddered again, not wanting to recall those dark days and that stupid emotional teenage threat made out of jealousy and anger, without thought for its consequences.

Even now, the memory of how easily it could all have gone dreadfully wrong haunted her. She had been criminally stupid, selfishly determined to vanquish Kyle once and for all, to ruin his triumphant homecoming from Oxford, and to make her parents choose between them.

And she had succeeded, but at what price?

Never would she forget the reproach and fear in her father's eyes when she'd woken up in her hospital room.

The indignity of having her stomach pumped out by the hospital staff had left her sore and exhausted, her brain not mentally capable of reasoning properly.

Her first croaked words had been, "Where's Kyle?"

And they had had the compassion and the love not to tell her then that he had gone.

It had all been so silly, her resentment of the fact that he'd chosen to return home on the very day of her birthday, and thus, in her eyes, taken the lime-light from her. She had refused to get changed for the special birthday dinner her parents had or-ganised at a local hotel, and instead had stayed up-stairs in her room sulking, sure that her father at least would come up and coax her to go down.

But it had been Kyle who had come up to see her. A Kyle older and far more mature than she'd remembered from his last visit, almost twelve months ago. During his last year at Oxford he had worked during his holidays and so they had not seen him, and she had managed to persuade herself that he was gone from their lives for ever, even though he wrote and telephoned regularly every week.

He had been curt and derisive with her, sparing her nothing, making her see herself as a spoiled, petulant child, determined to make everyone dance to her bidding. She had hated him even more for that, because she had seen in his coolly deliberate criticism the seeds of the truth, and that had hurt.

She had reacted wildly, close to the point of tears at what she considered her parents' betrayal of her in choosing to let him come up and torment her, when they should have sent him packing and spent the evening coaxing her out of her black mood.

'If you have the slightest bit of feeling for your parents, you'll get dressed and come downstairs right now,' Kyle had told her, getting off her bed. 'It's time you grew up, Heather, and stopped trying to use emotional blackmail to get what you want. OK, so you and I are always going to be poles apart, but for your parents' sake we should at least try to appear to get on.'

She had hated him for his calm, reasoned argument, for the realisation that he was showing more concern for her parents than she was herself; and all the nebulous and real fears she had experienced in the years since he had become an adopted member of her family had exploded inside her.

She'd refused to get dressed, and in the end her parents and Kyle had gone out without her.

Nearly demented with rage and jealousy that this should happen on her birthday, she had flown to the medicine cabinet and extracted a full bottle of aspirin.

She hadn't really wanted to die, just to punish those who should have loved her more than they did Kyle . . . much more.

If it hadn't been for the fact that Kyle had persuaded her parents to return home half-way through the meal, she would not be here today.

She'd been unconscious when they'd found her hysterical note. She had been rushed to hospital, and brought round by the unsympathetic and very angry hospital staff, who quite rightly felt that their time was far too valuable to be spent on one silly, jealous teenager, when there were so many other people in greater need of it.

She had said many bitter and angry things in her letter: accusing her parents of wishing she had been a boy, accusing Kyle of trying to steal their love away from her, and finally saying that, since she wasn't wanted or loved, she might as well end her life.

During the counselling she had received after her release from hospital, she had come to understand that it had not been Kyle she had hated so much as the threat she'd thought he represented; and that it was her own nature that was responsible for her feelings, rather than anything he had done.

She had been angry and resentful at these assertions, and then later, when she had come to understand the reality of them, very penitent. But by then it was too late. Kyle had disappeared, leaving only a note saying that in the circumstances, although he would always love and be grateful to them, he felt it would be as well if he didn't see her parents again.

His absence was never mentioned, but Heather knew how much her parents missed him. Her mother could have leaned on Kyle's strength, while her father could have turned to him for financial advice. If only...

But life wasn't a fairy story. It wasn't possible to simply close one's eyes and wish.

There was another way, though. Her mouth went dry at the very thought of it. It had been in her mind since her father had first been taken ill. She kept trying to dismiss it, to find another way out of her dilemma, but deep down inside she knew there was no other way.

Call it reparation for an old wrong, call it a test she had to face before being able to call herself fully adult, call it what you liked, it all boiled down to the same thing.

She had to go and see Kyle; she had to ask for his help on her parents' behalf. She had to humble and abase herself before him; she *had* to have his help.

She was out for longer than she had intended, and when she got back the phone was ringing again. She raced to answer it, tensing as she heard her mother's familiar but anxious voice.

'It's all right, darling. There's not been any change. Your father is still holding his own, but Mr Frazer has confirmed that he will have to have an operation. There's one surgeon in particular who's highly skilled in this particular surgery, but he's very much in demand. He's in New York at the moment, apparently, but he's due back at the end of the week. I've told Mr Frazer that we can't possibly afford a private operation, but he's asked me to talk to Mr Edmondson anyway. If only your father hadn't had to let his medical insurance lapse.'

Heather clutched the receiver, echoing her mother's thoughts, but money had been so tight this last year. She wondered if her mother knew about the bank mortgage her father had taken out on the house so that he would have some capital to inject into the business. The bank was already pressing for its payment, and once they knew her father was ill . . .

She shivered inwardly. Added stress at this particular moment in time was the very last thing her parents needed. She couldn't forget that, when she'd found her father, he had been slumped across his desk where he had been studying a depressingly long list of outstanding debts.

'I'm going to stay here tonight. The hospital has found me a room for as long as I need one. How are you . . . are you coping?'

How like her mother to be concerned for her, Heather reflected. How on earth had she ever managed to convince herself that her parents didn't care? All right, so maybe they would both have loved another child, especially a boy. They had loved Kyle, she acknowledged that, but their love for him had never diminished their love for her, although she herself had been too jealous and angry to see that.

'I'm fine. I'm working on the decorations for the church hall. I'll have to go to our suppliers tomorrow, I've run out of some stuff I need,' she added on sudden impulse. 'I'll be out for most of the day, so don't worry if you can't reach me.'

'Well, just be careful if you're driving,' her mother warned her, accepting her lie at face value. 'They're forecasting heavy frost for tonight, with snowfalls in the morning.'

Heather felt guilty as she hung up. She hated lying, but she needed time for what she had in mind, and not just time to accomplish her self-imposed task, but time to psyche herself up into carrying it out.

CHAPTER TWO

HEATHER slept badly, waking well before dawn and then lying in bed watching the darkness give way to light. An ominous faint pink flush tinged the sky, a threat of snow to come. Her sleep had been tormented by dreams that were made up of old memories and fears: Kyle's arrival, and the shock of his reality. He had been so much bigger than she had expected, and so very aggressive towards her. That aggression had been his only means of defence in an alien situation, she knew this now from her counselling. He had grown up in one of the toughest areas of London, deserted by his father and then left to the care of elderly grandparents when his mother had died at twenty-five from the results of an illegal abortion that went wrong. He had probably never known real kindness in his life before her parents came into it, she realised with hindsight. He was only one of several grandchildren cared for by his grandparents for one reason or another, and whereas the others had living parents he had not, and after his mother's death his grandparents had been more than happy to hand him over into state care.

He had been in and out of several children's homes since he was five, and had earned himself the reputation of being hard to control, and below normal intelligence.

What on earth had made her parents pick him out as a potential foster child, Heather still didn't know. To talk about him now was to enter forbidden and mined territory. Her parents missed him still; she only had to remember how her father had asked for him in those first minutes after he had recovered consciousness to know that, but out of love and fear for her they pretended he did not exist. It was a constant ache within her that she had allowed her own insecurity and jealousy to be the cause of so much hurt to them, but it was too late to go back now, too late to re-write the past.

But not too late to alter the future, she reminded herself, shivering a little as thoughts she didn't want to contemplate filled her mind.

Just as he had known she hated and resented him, so Kyle seemed to know that her parents genuinely loved him. It had soon been discovered that, far from being backward, he was actually of above a ˙rage intelligence. Her father, delighted with the quickness of his brain, ha organised special coaching for him; and when he won a scholarship to a local public school, they had been intensely proud of him.

Her last memory of him had been the fateful night of her seventeenth birthday. He had filled out during his time at university, his shoulders broad enough now to match his six-foot-odd physique. His skin had still been tanned from his working vacation abroad, and his black hair had curled strongly into his collar. He had brought into the femininity of her room a male essence that she had instinctively disliked. She could vividly remember how her whole body had almost quivered in response to it, as hatred for him filled her.

It was no good re-running the past, she couldn't alter what lay there, and there was no escape to be found down those avenues. There was something she had to do, a debt she owed her parents that must be repaid. A debt of love and sacrifice which she was surely now mature enough to give back.

She looked down at the piece of paper beside her bed. Yesterday she had looked up the head office address of Bennett Enterprises. To her surprise, it was in Bath. Less far away than she had thought. She had written it down, but there had been no need, it was practically burned into her brain.

She had it all planned. Her stomach muscles tightened tensely. What if he refused to even speak to her? What if he wasn't there?

Already she was looking for ways out, but for her parents' sake she had to go on.

She showered and dressed, agonising over what to wear to create the best impression, to show him how much she had grown and matured.

In the end she plumped for an elegant black jersey wool dress. It had been expensive and looked it, she admitted ruefully, as she zipped it up. It had been a 'thank you' present from someone for whom she had done some interior decoration schemes some months ago. She had enjoyed the challenge of the unexpected task and had flatly refused to take any money. The dress had been a surprise present, and one she had not had the heart to give back. It suited her, showing off her lean, narrow, feminine waist and the soft curves of her body.

Over it she wore a loose silk-effect coat with huge silver buttons and odd lace appliqués. It was the handiwork of a fellow art college friend, and against the rich darkness of her red hair she knew the black looked good.

For once her curls had obeyed the dictates of her brush, and lay smooth and controlled. Too nervous to eat, she made herself a cup of coffee, estimating how long it would take her to get to Bath.

The van they used for company business was her only means of transport, as her mother had their one and only car. The van was old but reliable, and she was used to driving it.

The threatened snow started to fall just before she reached the outskirts of Bath, reminding her that the brakes on the van needed checking. Grimacing faintly at the thought of the additional expense, she found somewhere to park.

There was just time for a calming cup of tea before she bearded the lion in his den. She headed for a favourite tea shop with a Dickensian ambience that surrounded its customers like a comforting favourite blanket.

The waitress recognised her, and gave her a beaming smile. Most of the customers seemed to be tourists, mainly Americans, Heather judged from their accents.

She poured her tea and drank it piping hot, trying to suppress the ever-increasing weight of memories.

When Kyle had been accepted at Oxford she had taunted him with the fact that his London accent would make him a laughing stock. It made her shudder to realise what a bitch she had been, but she had still been a child, and children did not fight by the rules. In point of fact, by that time he had had little trace of the very shrill Cockney accent he had had on first coming to them. Kyle, giving as good as he got, had said nothing at the time but, during their evening meal that night, in full earshot of her parents, he had mimicked her own voice, complete with the soft Dorset burr she had picked up at school. Of course, she had been bitterly humiliated, just as he had intended. She had still had to learn in those days that Kyle could outmatch her in almost every skill there was.

She realised her cup was empty and gave a faint sigh. It couldn't be put off any longer. Resolutely she got up and paid her bill.

Outside, it was still snowing. Her coat wasn't really designed as a protection against winter weather, and she shivered a little as she hurried in the direction of Kyle's offices.

She knew roughly where they were and, given that she was familiar with the nature of his work from the many newspaper articles published on him, she shouldn't have been surprised by the carefully restored Georgian façade of the building, nor the discretion of the small brass plate outside, announcing that within were the offices of Bennett Enterprises Limited.

Even in his choice of name for his company Kyle had to be different, she thought wryly. Any other young man starting out as a speculative builder and developer would have chosen something like Bennett Builders Limited, but not Kyle; even then he had seen his building company only as a cornerstone on which to build and expand.

Now his company was known as one of the most forward-thinking and responsible building firms around. His architects were called in whenever important restoration work was required, his expertise sought when the planners were at their wits' end on how to appease both the conservationists and the needs of an ever-growing population.

Recently he had branched out into sheltered accommodation for retired people, and by all accounts was proving as successful in that field as he had been in so many others.

At twenty-nine, he had a reputation for being one of the country's shrewdest and richest entrepreneurs.

For almost a moment Heather dithered, longing to turn tail and run, and yet held there by a stubborn desire to do what she knew was the right thing. This was her chance to make amends. To show that finally she had grown up and that the lessons learned from the months of counselling she had undergone after her attempted suicide had brought some return. That finally she had come to accept that love could be shared; that Kyle never had and never could be a threat to her own place in her parents' hearts.

In the end, it was the cold that drove her inside the building; that and the fact that she was attracting curious looks from busy passers-by.

Inside, her heels tapped noisily on the black and white marble-tiled floor; so noisily, in fact, that she was rather surprised that every one of the five doors leading off the rectangular entrance hall did not immediately open.

On either side of the hallway, between the two sets of doors, stood elegant console tables with matching mirrors hung over them. The Georgian period had always been a favourite of hers, and Heather recognised the value of the antique mirrors almost at a glance.

Attractive dried floral displays, in keeping with the winter season, decorated the tables, but it was only when she headed rather nervously for the stairs that one of the doors actually opened.

She must, she realised, as a uniformed com-missionaire politely enquired her business, having triggered off some sort of silent alarm.

She told him rather hesitantly that she had come to see Kyle Bennett, and then felt ridiculously foolish when she was forced to admit she was here without making an appointment. Plainly, that was simply not the sort of thing one did when ap-proaching the head of Bennett Enterprises, and she felt a tiny surge of well-remembered resentment start up inside her.

She almost turned to go, but then remembered why she had come here in the first place. Almost in desperation, she said hurriedly, 'Look, if I could write a note, could it be sent up to Ky—to Mr Bennett?'

That small slip in almost using Kyle's Christian name was making the commissionaire eye her even more suspiciously, and she stiffened when she re-alised that the man suspected that she was one of Kyle's cast-off girlfriends.

Even as a teenager he'd seemed to have had a fatal fascination that attracted members of her sex, and since he had become successful the gossip columns had regularly mentioned his name, connecting it with a variety of pretty socialites and would-be models-cum-actresses.

Surely one glance at her had been enough to inform the commissionaire that she was scarcely the type to attract the great Kyle Bennett, Heather thought bitterly.

'Mr Bennett knows my...parents,' she told him coldly. 'If I could just write that note...'

'In here, miss.'

The commissionaire obviously believed her, because his manner relaxed slightly as he showed her into one of the empty downstairs rooms.

Obviously a waiting-room of sorts, it was decorated with watered-silk wall hangings, the Georgian panels painted in a chinoiserie design of birds and branches. Two deep-cushioned settees were covered in the same pastel watered silk as the walls, a cheerful open fire burned in what Heather suspected must be the original Adam grate, and the commissionaire escorted her over to a pretty early Victorian writing-desk, fully equipped with notepaper and pens.

She wrote quickly, before she could change her mind, feeling the desperation and dislike building up inside her as she did so. When she had finished, she studied what she had written for a second.

'Kyle, I need to talk to you about Mum and Dad. Please don't ignore this note.'

And she sighed it with her full name.

She sealed it before she could give way to any second thoughts, and handed it to the waiting man.

Once he had gone she was seized by a wave of dread, so strong that she was actually half-way to the door before she realised what she was doing. She couldn't leave now. She had to see this thing through. What was she frightened of? Making a fool of herself in front of Kyle, laying herself open to his mockery and contempt? Was her own pride really so important that it mattered more to her than her father's life?

Instantly ashamed, she went back into the room. The very worst thing Kyle could do would be to refuse to see her. It didn't matter how much he humiliated her, as long as he agreed to pay for her father's operation.

For the first time she contemplated what was likely to happen if her mission failed. The thought made her skin go cold, and she started to shiver.

The commissionaire, walking in and seeing her, frowned and asked anxiously, 'Are you all right, miss?'

'Yes, yes . . . I'm fine.' Heather gave him a distracted smile. She was so tensed up that her body was aching with the strain she was imposing on it.

'Mr Bennett said to show you up.'

Was she imagining that new tinge of respect in the man's voice? Plainly the man thought she had been given something approaching an accolade, but she could not allow herself to relax yet. All she had achieved was one tiny step forward.

The lift was hidden away discreetly, behind another of the doors. As it slid smoothly upwards, Heather pressed a protesting hand to her taut stomach. She was only just beginning to realise the true meaning of the phrase 'butterflies in the tummy'. The ones in hers seemed to be involved in a mad, frantic dance.

The lift stopped and, following the commission-aire's directions, she walked down the elegantly decorated corridor to its solitary door.

It was opened before she reached it, and the young woman who motioned her in made Heather all too aware of the shortcomings in her own face and figure. This girl could have posed from the front cover of *Vogue* and drawn gasps of awe from everyone who saw her.

She was a perfect, frosted Nordic blonde of the type normally found in sophisticated American cities, cool and very sure of herself, her glance sweeping dismissively over Heather's now tousled curls and clothes.

The simple little outfit she was wearing looked very like a Donna Karan, the silk jersey fluidly tracing every lush curve of her perfect figure. Her nails, medium length and impossibly glossy, re-proached the lack of attention Heather paid to hers. It was impossible to keep them immaculate when she was working, and instinctively she tucked them away in her pockets.

'Kyle said to show you straight in.'

Her smile revealed perfectly capped teeth, her accent pure Sloane Ranger, whose whole manner was designed to intimidate, Heather reflected as she followed her through an ante-room and up to a heavy panelled door.

She tapped on it and then pushed it open, standing aside so that Heather could go in.

It was furnished exactly as she might have expected, all stripped-down panels and a huge status-symbol desk, behind which she expected to find Kyle sitting.

Only he wasn't. He was standing in front of the fire, engaged in the homely task of putting fresh logs on it.

He turned round as his secretary closed the door, dusting off his hands, his cool eyes taking their time in surveying her.

'Well, this *is* a surprise.'

There was nothing in his manner to give her any clue as to how he was going to react to her request. She had half expected a sarcasm that wasn't there, but the lack of it only made her skin prickle with increased nervousness.

She had forgotten how magnetic he was, how he dominated every situation he was in, simply by the power of his personality. No man who had made of his life what he had, from the very worst of beginnings, could have achieved so much without it, but she had forgotten, or overlooked, how awe-inspiring he could be.

The immaculate dark suit and crisp white shirt added to the image, of course. His tie was discreet, and toned beautifully with his suit. When he shot back his cuff and glanced frowningly at his watch, as though warning her that her time was limited, she caught a flash of gold against the snowy white, and the firelight played momentarily on the sinewy strength of his wrist, his flesh brown and firm, criss-crossed with a dark feathering of hairs. Her stomach somersaulted and she was shaken by a sudden surge of inexplicable reaction. She wanted to turn tail and run, and probably would have done so, if he hadn't moved, fragmenting the image burned on her brain.

'Your note said you wanted to see me about your parents.'

His voice hadn't changed, although now all trace of his accent seemed to have been obliterated. It had almost gone that last time he had come home, she remembered, surprised by the sudden shudder the sound of it sent off deep inside her.

He had moved, so that he was blocking the heat of the fire from her, and suddenly she realised how cold she was. She could feel the shivers building up inside her, her fingers icy-cold, in direct contrast to the heat she could feel filling her cheeks and throat.

It was just tension, she told herself, that was all. And yet, even knowing what was causing her physical symptoms, she still found it very disconcerting to have to acknowledge the physical effect he was having on her.

'It's Dad,' she blurted out, desperate to say what she had come to say and get away. 'He's very ill. He's had a bad heart attack. The specialist says he needs open-heart surgery and a bypass operation.'

She looked directly at him for the first time since she had come into the room, her white pallor broken only by the two over-bright patches of hectic colour in her cheeks.

'We can't afford it, and the waiting list on the NHS is so long that Dad could well be dead before he can have the operation.'

'What are you asking me for, Heather?' Kyle's eyebrows rose, his mouth twisting sardonically, and she felt the old familiar flare of dislike rise up inside her. Strange to think of that hard mouth being pressed to a woman's in passion. She shuddered deeply, stunned by the uncharted direction of her thoughts, the heat in her face increasing. What stupid tricks were her mind playing on her now? Kyle's sex life was the last thing she could be thinking about.

'Shall I make a guess?'

The smooth drawl brought her back to reality, her head snapping back as she looked at him.

'You want me to pay for the operation, is that it? You want money from me, in other words . . . a cash payment for the years you had to put up with me in your home. What price have you put on that intrusion, Heather, or haven't you worked it out yet?'

She almost choked in her rage, aching to retaliate and fly at him as she had ached to do so often as a child. Why was it he had the power to rile her like this? Why was it he seemed to know exactly how to find her Achilles' heel?

'How much do you want, Heather?'

He had turned away from her, but she could still hear the weary cynicism in his voice, and suddenly she knew that nothing . . . nothing could make her beg from this man.

'Nothing,' she told him bitterly. 'I don't want anything from you, Kyle. I thought you cared about my parents. I know they still love you. I know that they still miss you, especially my father... You were the first person he asked for when he finally regained consciousness. He was confused, you see,' she told him, her throat tight with pain and her own bitter remorse. 'He had forgotten that you'd left us.'

The tears that filled her eyes flowed on to her face and she dashed them away impatiently, too caught up in her own feelings of inadequacy and pain to care any longer how she might demean herself.

'They love you, Kyle, and I love them, and when I saw my father lying there in intensive care I wished with all my heart that I could wipe out the past, that I could...' She broke off, horrified with herself and what she was betraying, but it was too late.

'Go on,' Kyle demanded grimly. 'What did you wish, Heather? That you hadn't been such a stupid, spoiled little brat? That you hadn't nearly destroyed your own life out of spite and jealousy?'

Anguish made her veil her eyes from him as the memories she had been fighting to suppress flooded back. It had always been like this between them. The very air in the room seemed fraught with tension and dislike. Why? They were both adults now. She knew that she had been more at fault than Kyle, but surely he could see, just as she had come to see, that each of them had been equally jealous of the other.

'My parents need you, Kyle,' she told him quietly, pride strengthening her voice as she added, 'not because you can pay for Dad's operation. If either of them knew I was here now, they would be furious. No, they need you because they miss you; because they need someone to lean on.' She took a deep breath and added shakily, meeting his brooding look head on, 'They need you because they love you.'

She couldn't interpret the look he gave her. The silence seemed to last for ever, broken only by the soft hiss of the burning logs. She looked blindly towards the window, sure that she had failed and that he was about to throw her out. Outside, it was still snowing and she shivered. What was the matter with her? She shouldn't be so cold. She felt hollow and empty inside, and she frowned, trying to remember when she had last had something to eat.

Her muscles ached from the control she was imposing on them; if she relaxed even for a second she would be quivering like a tormented child.

'I'll ask you again,' Kyle said softly. 'What is it you want from me, Heather?'

He hadn't thrown her out; she could hardly believe it. Relief made her muscles go weak, the hiss of the logs sank echoingly in her ears, and her own voice seemed to reach her through a vast echoing chamber as she replied huskily, 'I want you to go and see Dad... You could pretend you'd heard about the heart attack from someone else. Please, Kyle... It would mean so much to him, to both of them. They miss you and I can't talk to them about it. They... they don't want to hurt me.'

She made the admission huskily, hating what she must be betraying to him, but although she tensed herself against it, strangely he made no attempt to probe deeper.

'And you want me to offer to pay for him to have his operation privately?'

'Yes,' she agreed baldly, 'but not because I think you owe them anything, Kyle. What they gave you, they gave freely. If you want to think of it in terms of a payment, then tell yourself it's payment to me for finally admitting what I've known for years, and refused to admit. That my parents love and need you, possibly more than they love and need me.'

There, she had said it. She couldn't endure any more. She couldn't wait for his reaction, for his possible cruelty. She turned and headed blindly for the door, desperately trying to blink away her tears.

'Heather.'

She winced and cried out beneath the fierce pressure of his fingers as they dug into her shoulders.

'For God's sake, I'm not going to hurt you. You can stop bristling like an angry cat,' Kyle told her curtly. 'I'm not going to hurt you.'

'You already have,' Heather retorted shakily, as he released her. Her shoulder felt bruised where he had grabbed hold of her, and as she moved it experimentally she saw him frown.

'You're almost skin and bone,' he told her flatly. 'What the devil have you been doing to yourself? Don't tell me you've discovered anorexia...'

The gibe hurt, all the more so because it could have been so pertinent. Had the slimmers' disease received its present-level publicity when she was a teenager, she could all too easily have used it as a form of blackmail against her parents, she suspected. Trust Kyle to see that and turn it to his own advantage.

'I'm an adult now, Kyle,' she told him stiffly. 'I don't play stupid games like that.'

He studied her in a way that was very unnerving.

'Yes, I forgot. You opted to undergo counselling after...'

'After I stupidly pretended I wanted to commit suicide, and it nearly all went wrong? You can say

the words, you know, Kyle. That's part of the
therapy. I don't try to hide away from what I did,
and yes, you're quite right, I did opt to undergo
counselling, and it did teach me a lot about myself
and my motives, as well as those of others...'

If he realised she was trying to retaliate, and break
through his own armour, he did not betray it.

'You're too thin,' he repeated, ignoring her
comment. 'You'll have to be careful, otherwise
you're going to end up looking haggard. How old
are you now? Twenty-four...five?'

He knew damn well she was only twenty-three,
Heather thought bitterly, and if he liked his women
as lushly curved as the elegant doll in his outside
office, then yes, she was too thin.

She said what she was thinking without monitoring her words, and was surprised by the attract-
iveness of the amused smile that slashed across his
face. She had forgotten those creases either side of
his mouth, had forgotten how maddeningly, physically compelling he could be when he wished. Possibly because he had never bothered to even try to
charm her, she acknowledged wryly.

'She's quite something, isn't she?' he agreed ap-
preciatively, and then asked blandly, 'Is there
anyone serious in your life at the moment, Heather,
or are you still playing at pretending to have a
career?'

The taunt hurt, particularly since she herself had
always felt that her father had manufactured her
job for her. It made no difference that she had flair
and a definite artistic talent, she still worked for
her father and was paid a salary the business could
not really afford.

'I came here to ask you to go and see my father, Kyle,' she told him coolly. 'Not to discuss my personal life. If you won't...'

She made to walk towards the door and then faltered when he made no move to stop her.

'Still the same old Heather,' he drawled cynically. 'Still trying to use emotional blackmail.'

Instantly, all her good intentions deserted her; her temper, always quick, flared to red-hot heat and she said fiercely, 'That's not true. I was *not* trying to blackmail you.' She turned round quickly, too quickly, she realised dizzily, as she felt the room start to spin and fade ominously around her.

She was aware of Kyle grabbing hold of her, and then forcing her down into one of the fireside chairs. She even heard him cursing her and calling her a stupid little fool, but for once she felt too confused to protest at the sensation of his hands on her body, pushing away her coat, reaching behind her to release the zip of her dress as he yanked her forward, so that her head flopped down, and she could feel the coldness of the air against her naked back.

The whole affair could only have lasted seconds. No sooner had Kyle pushed her head down than she felt the dizziness start to clear and full awareness return. She sat up immediately, furious to discover that he had lowered her zip so much that she couldn't reach it without contorting herself.

'Stop struggling... I'll do it for you.'

She tensed beneath the cool firmness of his hand on her back. She could feel his breath against her skin, and to her shock the warmth of it raised a betraying rash of small goose-bumps.

'No holiday this year,' he remarked casually as he closed the zip for her. 'Or don't you believe in exposing such pale skin to the sun's rays?'

His comment, although impersonal, threw her; she wasn't used to the intimacy of having a man's hands on her body, and his comment seemed a further intrusion into her privacy.

'My skin doesn't tan. I should have thought you'd remember that,' she snapped bitterly, remembering the one summer she had tried to outdo his almost permanent golden-brown skin, and had practically given herself third degree burns.

Her body had swelled up and her skin had flamed painful scarlet. And, as if that hadn't been enough, she had been diabolically sick, and had had to stay indoors for almost a week with the curtains closed, and her mother constantly applying calamine lotion.

'Your skin will be like leather by the time you're forty,' she added acidly.

'While yours will still feel like the most expensive kind of silk velvet.'

It took several seconds for his comment to sink in, and when it did she turned and stared open-mouthed at him, her shock registering in the rounded darkness of her amber eyes.

'What's wrong, Heather? Surely you're used to men commenting on the delicate quality of your skin. Your lovers...'

His voice was having a curious effect on her senses. She had never had him speak to her in that soft, caressing tone before, and apprehension flared to life inside her as she tried to reject its effect.

The images he was conjuring up shocked her. She felt tongue-tied with a mixture of embarrassment and fury, and although she was unaware of it her eyes had darkened as they always did when she was either disturbed or afraid.

'I've already told you, I didn't come here to talk about my private life, Kyle...'

'As I understand it, there isn't much to talk about.'

He straightened up and carried on before she could digest the full import of his words. 'I will go and see your father, Heather. When I've seen him, you and I will probably need to talk again. Are you free to lunch with me tomorrow? I have to fly to the States the day after to see a potential client.'

What could she say? She had to agree, and she was half-way back to the van before she realised exactly what Kyle had said to her before making that lunch appointment. She stopped dead in her tracks, aware of the black looks her unexpected action was earning her from people forced to avoid colliding with her.

How could Kyle know anything about her personal life? It had been six years since they had last met, and yet he had spoken with such authority, such confidence—almost as though he knew all there was to know about her. But how could that be? Unless... unless he had been keeping tabs on them. She frowned. But if that had been the case he would already have known about her father. Frowning now, she tried to recall if he had shown any reaction to her announcement, but Kyle had always been good at keeping his feelings to himself.

Besides, she had been far too tense and wrought up to pay much attention to how he was looking.

She had achieved what she had hoped for, or at least the first part of it. She ought to be feeling triumphant and relieved, but she wasn't. She didn't want Kyle Bennet back in their lives, not in any capacity; and yet, for her parents' sake, she knew she would have to endure him. If he allowed himself to become a part of their lives. There was always the chance that he would go back on his word, or perhaps just visit her father, and leave it at that.

Whatever happened, her parents must never know that she had prompted his visit. They would hate that. No, that must remain her secret, hers and Kyle's. It gave her an odd feeling to know that she shared something with him from which her parents were excluded.

CHAPTER THREE

THE snow, which had not lain particularly deeply on the road in Bath itself, thickened once Heather was clear of the city, although fortunately it had stopped falling. The van was old and inclined to be temperamental, and by the time she got home Heather was suffering from the most excruciating tension headache.

She knew that she ought to have something to eat, but the thought of food was totally nauseating. Instead, she made herself a strong cup of coffee and sat down in the old kitchen chair that the cats thought of as their special preserve. Hilda, the oldest of them, a farm tabby of immense dignity, glared balefully at her and then vented her ire on Meg, spitting at the dog as she sat down at Heather's side.

Was she cushioned from reality living here with her parents? It was an almost idyllic existence for anyone who felt the way she did about the country-side; her work was not particularly arduous, and certainly could never be compared with the rat-race suffered by those who had to commute every day to cities like London. Without putting his scorn into words, Kyle had still managed to imply that he found her contemptible; or was it just her own in-tense sensitivity where he was concerned that made her question herself like this? Kyle had remarked that the business was barely able to support her parents, never mind providing a salary for her as well. That had been quite true, but what he could not know was that recently she had found herself shouldering more and more of the responsibility for the company. Her father had complained of feeling tired, and now she berated herself for not questioning him more deeply, for not seeing that his lack of enthusiasm was a pointer to his physical vulnerability.

She wasn't a complete fool. She knew that the business was slowly going downhill, that the work was going to be too much for her father, and yet, without the business, how could her parents possibly survive?

Her anxiety drove her to abandon her comfortable chair in the kitchen and go instead to the small, cold backroom they used as an office. Once there, she opened the desk drawer that held the company's books.

It took the lack of light in the small room to make her realise how long she had spent there. Raising her head, she massaged the back of her neck tiredly. It made no difference which way she did the calculations; they were still perilously close to the edge of bankruptcy. *Why* had her father never told her about the mortgage he had taken out on the house? She closed her eyes, alarmingly near to tears, longing for someone to confide in and hand her worries over to, and yet at the same time knowing that there was nothing anyone could do to help.

It was almost four o'clock. Soon her mother would be ringing, and she had promised that she would go round to the village hall tonight and help to put up the decorations.

Almost on cue, the phone rang, but to her shock it wasn't her mother on the other end of the line, but Kyle Bennett. She was so stunned that it was several seconds before she could speak.

'Not still sulking with me because I told you a few home truths, are you?' Kyle asked her dulcetly, and instantly her fatigue vanished and anger burned through her.

'You've got the wrong woman, Kyle,' she told him crisply. 'I don't sulk. What do you want?'

'I've got a couple of tickets for the *Phantom*. I thought you might like to see it.'

The total unexpectedness of his invitation took her breath away. She remembered reading somewhere that tickets for the fantastic *Phantom of the Opera* show were impossible to find and, if she was honest with herself, she would have loved to go, but not with Kyle.

'I'm sorry, I can't,' she told him, not without a certain amount of satisfaction. 'I've got something else on tonight.'

There was a long pause, during which Heather had time to ask herself why Kyle should want to take her out and to wonder exactly what sort of macabre game he was playing with her. Then he said, sardonically, 'I see... where will you finish your evening off, I wonder, his place or yours? It must cramp your style, surely, living at home. Or do you make sure that all your lovers...'

She had slammed down the receiver before she had thought about what she was doing. She was literally shaking with rage and chagrin. How dared Kyle infer that she was making use of her father's illness to bring a man home? How dared he imply...

Shakily she sat down, trying to calm herself. He was not deliberately trying to taunt her, she told herself, he was simply assuming that she lived her life in the same way that he lived his.

Not even the peacefulness of her tea-time walk with Meg had the power to fully restore her to normal.

Her mother rang when she got back to say that her father was making slow progress. They chatted for a while and then she rang off. As she replaced the receiver, Heather frowned. There was a note of constraint in her mother's voice, almost as though she was concealing something from her. Her heartbeat increased in tempo, her skin chilling with fear. Could her father be worse than she thought? She looked at the phone, longing to pick it up and call her mother back, and yet knowing she couldn't.

Despite her concern the evening passed quickly. Mrs Anstey had a nephew staying with her who came down to the hall to help them. He was in the army and on leave from Germany, a very pleasant man in his late twenties, with a slightly old-fashioned, rather courtly manner that was undeniably attractive. He was nothing like as physically attractive as Kyle, and yet there was something about him that made her feel protected and safe, Heather decided, warming more and more to him as the evening went by.

She had walked down to the village, and when he offered to drive her back she accepted with alacrity.

It was only a short drive, and she felt obliged to invite him in for a cup of coffee. While she was in the kitchen making it, she heard the phone ring.

'Could you answer it for me?' she called out. 'It will probably be my mother.'

He already knew all about her father's collapse from his aunt, and as Heather poured the heated milk into their mugs she heard him lift the receiver.

'It isn't your mother,' he told her, coming into the kitchen. 'It's some chap called Bennett.'

Heather almost dropped the pan. *Kyle,* ringing her again? Howard was frowning slightly, his manner slightly withdrawn, almost disapproving, she recognised, bewildered by his sudden volte-face.

'I don't think I'll stay for coffee, if you don't mind. I'm off early in the morning... Nice meeting you . . .'

He was gone before she could raise a protest, leaving her to hurry to the telephone and pick up the receiver.

'Who's the boyfriend?' demanded Kyle.

'Howard is the nephew of a friend of my parents, not that it's any business of yours,' Heather told him freezingly, adding unwillingly, 'What on earth did you say to him? He wouldn't even stay for a cup of coffee!'

Kyle ignored her question and continued laconically, 'I've been to the hospital and seen your father.'

Instantly Howard was forgotten.

'You have? Kyle, tell me the truth, how is he? Mum sounded very constrained when she rang me earlier. I'm sure there's something she's keeping from me.'

There was an odd pause, and then he said cynically, 'You *have* changed, haven't you? The Heather

I remember was far too wrapped up in her own personal grievances to notice what anyone else felt.'

The taunt was probably justified, but hurt nevertheless.

'Your father is holding his own, Heather, but, as you told me, he's got to have further surgery as quickly as possible. I've spoken to your mother about it, and we've agreed on what we think is the best plan of action. Your mother will ring you later. By the way, she's given me permission to go over the company's books. It seems the business is on your father's mind. He's worrying about it, and she thinks that if I go through the books it will help ease his mind.'

The implication being that *she* did not have the intelligence to deal with them, Heather thought, hurt by her mother's lack of faith in her.

'I'll bring them tomorrow when we have lunch.'

'No, I'd like to have them tonight. I'll come over for them now, if that's all right, and then we can discuss them together tomorrow when we talk about your father's treatment.

Heather was too taken aback to protest, managing only a weak, 'Kyle, it's very late. I was just about to go to bed...'

'Alone, I trust,' he taunted suavely.

'It seems I don't have much choice,' Heather retorted freezingly, remembering the way Howard had so quickly and unflatteringly left.

'Disappointed?'

'Hardly, as I had no intention of going to bed with him in any case. Some of us have far more concern for our health than to indulge in emotionally meaningless sexual gratification, Kyle.'

She was quite pleased with that one, and was glad he couldn't see the chagrin she knew must be on her face when he retorted smoothly, 'I quite agree. Anyone who indulges in sex these days without due regard for their partner's past history must either be criminally stupid or have a death wish. I'll be over within the hour,' he concluded without giving her an opportunity to object. 'If you could have everything ready for me?'

The switch from tormentor to businessman confused her, and she found that she had said goodbye and replaced the receiver, without so much as a murmur.

Since she had to wait up for Kyle, she might as well use the time, Heather decided, gathering up the materials she would need for a small order from a local boutique.

The girl who ran it had been at the same school as her. She was married now, with two small children. Her husband had left her during the summer, and this boutique was to be both a means of earning her living and supporting her children, and something to occupy her thoughts and time.

Her husband's desertion had left her bitter and angry; they had been teenage sweethearts and had married when she was just eighteen. Now she was twenty-five, still only young, but with two small children to support she had responsibilities that had aged her emotionally, if not physically.

'When these two grow up,' she'd told Heather, the last time she had visited her, looking at her small daughters, 'I'm going to tell them not to fall into the same trap as I did. *And* I'm going to make sure that they have some means of supporting themselves. I've been lucky, my parents have set me up in this shop, but I know other girls my age in similar circumstances who have nothing to live on other than haphazard maintenance payments when their husbands are feeling either generous or guilty, and their state benefit. Have you any idea how much it costs to buy a child a decent pair of shoes?' she had complained.

Heather had promised to create something unusual for her Christmas window, and although the commission wouldn't bring much in in the way of cash, it would give her something to do with her hands while she waited for Kyle.

The last time he had been here had been the night . . . but no, she wasn't going to torture herself by going all through that again.

The phone rang abruptly, cutting through her thoughts. She picked up the receiver, not really surprised to hear her mother's voice.

'Heather, you'll never guess what! *Kyle* came to see your father tonight. Apparently he'd heard about . . . about him being ill, somehow or other, and he came down to the hospital to see him.' Her voice faltered suddenly. 'Darling, are you still there?'

Gripping the receiver, Heather forced a smile into her voice as she responded, 'I'm still here. You must have been happy to see him.'

There was a pause, during which she sensed her mother's hesitation.

'I should have waited until you came in to see your father to tell you, darling, but we were both so surprised to see him.'

'Mum, I'm all grown up now. I don't resent Kyle any more. I've come to terms with my jealousy of him, and I'm delighted that he's been in touch with you.'

Over the distance that separated them she felt her mother's relief. After a brief pause she hurried on, breathlessly, 'He's offered to give us whatever help we need. Oh, Heather, it's such a relief! I've been so worried... Kyle's promised to come with me when I go to see the specialist...'

Jealousy, sharp and piercing, twisted inside her, and she fought it down. She had taught herself to deal with this years ago, and she wasn't going to give in to it now.

'Dad must have been thrilled,' she interrupted, putting as much enthusiasm and warmth into her voice as she could. 'I know how he's missed Kyle... how you've both missed him.'

'He should be getting in touch with you. I was saying how worried we were about the business, and he's offered to go through the books for us. You don't mind, do you, darling?'

The anxiety and concern in her mother's voice stilled her jealousy.

'No, of course I don't,' she lied. 'I'll have the books ready for him...'

'I know how you feel about him, darling, but... Oh, I've got to go, there's someone else wanting to use the phone. I'll ring you tomorrow.'

There had been no disguising the happiness in her mother voice. Face it, Heather, she told herself fiercely. They *do* love him, not more than they love you, perhaps, but in a different way. You've always known that, and now's the time when you finally prove to yourself that you've actually grown up.

Her parents needed someone to lean on, she knew that. They needed someone who could remove from their shoulders the burden and responsibility of their failing business and, although she hated it, that someone could not be her.

She was still working an hour later when she heard Kyle's car drive up.

It was gone eleven, and she wondered what their neighbours down the quiet country lane would make of his arrival. By tomorrow it would be all round the village that she had been entertaining a man in her parents' absence. She smiled wryly to herself. There was nothing malicious about the village grapevine, and once she had explained who her late visitor was the gossip would quickly die down. Most of the villagers would remember Kyle, and his reappearance would be greeted with the same tactful lack of comment that had been their reaction to her own folly all those years ago. The village was a community that believed in protecting its own, and she had never been made to feel uncomfortable about what she had done.

Perhaps that was why she liked living here so much; she enjoyed the feeling of being part of an extended family. City life, with its pressures and aloneness, was not for her. Not for the first time, as she went to let Kyle in, she wondered a little at her own lack of driving ambition.

The casual jeans and sweater he was wearing should have made him look less imposing, but somehow they didn't. He was a man who did not need expensive clothes to make one aware of his power, Heather realised, as she stepped back instinctively when confronted by him.

'Still the same old Heather,' he goaded softly. 'Still retreating into your own safe space and giving off "keep off" signs.'

'I've got the books ready for you,' she told him shortly, turning her back on him.

'What a welcome. Don't I even get offered a cup of coffee?'

He was already making his way toward the kitchen, and Heather felt the old familiar antagonism spike through her.

'I didn't think you'd want to waste time drinking coffee. Not when it was so imperative that you have the books tonight.'

'I told you, I want to go through them before we lunch tomorrow. Forget the coffee, if that's how you feel.'' He shrugged, and as he moved Heather saw that he actually looked tired and strained.

Guilt attacked her. Kyle *did* love her parents, and his love was a stronger, more altruistic caring than her own. She knew that, and she hated the way he made her feel small-minded and mean.

'There's some made. I'll heat up some milk.'

Although he said nothing, she saw the tightening of his mouth at her curt response.

The moment he walked into the kitchen Meg greeted him with an ecstatic welcome. She obviously remembered him, and again Heather had to conquer a ridiculous surge of jealousy.

'Here's your coffee.' She put it down. 'I'll just go and get the books.'

When she brought them back he was stretched out in the chair, his eyes closed. What was it about seeing such a powerful-looking man so apparently vulnerable that brought an odd lump to her throat?

Hurriedly she cleared her throat, and immediately his head lifted. She handed him the folders and he put them down, quickly checking through them.

'There doesn't seem to be an order book here.'

'Oh, it's upstairs... I'll go and get it.'

It was in her room. She had taken it up with her last night when she'd gone to bed.

She didn't realise that Kyle had followed her upstairs until she opened the door to her room.

She had recently completed redecorating it, using oddments of fabric and wallpapers she had picked up at bargain prices. Stencils which she had designed and painted herself broke up the starkness of the plain walls, and she had experimented on her old furniture with dragging and marbling techniques to achieve what she rather proudly felt was an extremely effective up-date.

'I see you've still got Charles.'

Kyle's voice behind her made her jump and spin round, her whole body bristling with resentment at his intrusion into her own private sanctum.

Charles was her old teddy bear, and he still held pride of place on her dressing-table. She had kept him purely out of sentiment, but now, seeing him through Kyle's yes, she saw him as a symbol of a stupidly childish woman who refused to grow up. Snatching him up, she pushed him behind a curtain.

'I wasn't criticising,' Kyle told her. 'I've still got the first present your folks ever gave me. A football.'

'I remember it . . .' She did indeed. She could remember the day she and her parents had gone out to buy it. They had been so excited about the prospect of Kyle coming to live with them permanently, and she had been resentful and determined to be as difficult as possible.

They had wanted to buy him a fort, complete with toy soldiers, but had finally settled on the football. They had bought her a doll, which she had never touched, she remembered, sighing for the stubborn, difficult child she had been.

'Heather . . .'

Was that really diffidence she could hear in his voice? Abruptly she turned away, not wanting to hear whatever it was he was going to say.

'Here's the full order book. We'd better go down, your coffee will be getting cold. Or would you like to have a look at your old room while we're up here, just for "old times' sake"?'

She bit her lip immediately she had made the sarcastic remark. What was the matter with her? Already she seemed to be doing her best to antagonise Kyle. She saw his mouth thin and tighten.

'Still the same old Heather, after all.'

The weary resignation she heard in his voice was so out of character that she stared at him.

'Kyle . . .'

'Forget it. I thought you'd finally grown up, Heather, but it seems I was wrong. I'll take all this stuff home with me and then we can discuss it over lunch tomorrow. How well do you know Bath?'

'Reasonably,' she responded, not sure where his question was leading.

'I own a property just outside the city. We'll meet there.'

Back in the kitchen he gave her the address and directions. Heather had a good idea where it was and assured him that she shouldn't have any problems in finding it.

'Good. I'll see you there about twelve.'

He got up and picked up all the files, leaving Heather to almost run after him as he headed for the door in long strides.

'Be careful when you're driving,' he warned her as she let him out. 'Frost and then more snow is forecast . . . just as well he decided to leave.'

The taunting note in his voice reminded her of Howard's hurried exit, and she demanded angrily, 'Just what exactly did you say to him?'

'What makes you think it was something *I* said? Perhaps he got scared and changed his mind. You've got a very hungry look about you, Heather. Some men might find that intimidating.'

'But not you, I suppose,' Heather challenged, too angry to watch her words.

'Are you trying to tell me that you actually want to find out?'

Of course she wasn't, and he knew it! This element of sexual tension had never been there in their previous relationship of mutual antipathy, and she couldn't understand how it came to be there now. It confused and alarmed her. She wasn't used to indulging in this kind of riposte with Kyle, and when he made comments like that it threw her. As he fully intended it should do, she suspected angrily.

While she hunted desperately to think up a suitably crushing retort, he was already turning to leave.

'I'll see you tomorrow,' were his last words to her.

CHAPTER FOUR

ODDLY, in view of her pending luncheon engagement with Kyle, Heather slept very well, but the moment she woke up her tension returned. Yesterday's headache was now just a vague nagging pain in the back of her neck and, while her concern over the financing of her father's operation had eased, she was now on edge in a different way.

She had told herself, from the moment she'd accepted that she would have to approach Kyle on her parents' behalf, that her memories of him were coloured by her own immaturity and jealousy, and that he could not be as all-powerful as she had imagined. It had been disturbing to discover how quickly and how easily he could make her feel fourteen years old again.

Today, though, he was not going to catch her off guard. She would be in full control. She would be calm and restrained, and they would talk about the business as though he was as remote from her personal life as her father's bank manager or accountant.

It worried her how quickly and easily he seemed to have slipped back into their lives. It was almost as though he had never been gone.

He made her feel like a cat with its fur stroked the wrong way, all on edge and ruffled.

Her skin was too pale, she acknowledged as she got ready. Too many sleepless nights and too much worry had taken their toll on her. She had lost weight; the skirt she had decided to wear was loose on her waist, her face looked drained and tired, and even her hair, normally so vibrant and full of life, seemed lacklustre.

An hour later, she stood back from her mirror and viewed her reflection critically. It was amazing what make-up could achieve. She hadn't gone to art school for nothing and, although there was nothing heavy or overdone about the way she had made up her face, she had subtly managed to conceal nearly all the effects of the last few very harrowing days.

It wasn't snowing when she left, although snow was forecast and it was bitterly cold. The roads were treacherous, with deep ruts of frozen slush and patches of ice.

The van had been slow to start, coughing and sputtering protestingly, and it seemed to Heather as she drove that the engine note didn't sound quite as it ought.

She drove slowly and carefully, not wanting to take any risks. She had allowed herself plenty of time, and Kyle's directions were very clear and concise.

He hadn't given her any explanation as to why he wanted her to call at his home, other than to say that sometimes he preferred to work from there. She had half expected to find him living in one of the many very lovely formal mansions in the countryside surrounding Bath, but instead, when she finally turned in through the gates and up the drive, she discovered in front of her a low, rambling farmhouse built in cream stone under a slate roof.

Kyle's car, a powerful Jaguar, stood outside, and although the informal gardens looked bare under the harsh winter sky Heather could well imagine that in spring and summer this must be an idyllic spot.

Kyle came out to greet her as she stopped the van.

If anything, the temperature seemed to have dropped even further. Or maybe it was just because she was so cold that she thought it had, for as they went inside Kyle remarked casually, glancing at the sky, 'We'll have snow before the afternoon's over. I can smell it in the air, can't you?'

She hadn't come here to listen to idle conversation about the weather, Heather thought tensely, as she allowed him to take her heavy coat.

The heating system in the van was temperamental to say the least, and she shivered as she took her coat off.

'Cold? Come into the library.'

The floor in the hallway was uneven and homely, huge polished stone slabs with rich dark rugs over them.

Kyle opened one of the doors and stood back to let her pass. The doorway was only narrow, and as she moved forward Heather caught the clean male scent of his skin. Instantly her muscles froze, a faint frisson of sensation skittering down her spine.

'What's the matter?'

She caught Kyle's frown as she hurried forward, her face flushing uncomfortably in the realisation of her almost sexual awareness of him.

'Just cold, that's all,' she fibbed, hurrying towards the fire burning in the huge stone grate.

On the carved wooden mantel she could see a coat of arms with a Latin inscription, and she pretended to be engrossed in it to give herself time to get back to normal. What was the matter with her? It was completely crazy that she should have imagined, even for a second, that that peculiar frisson had been caused by anything remotely sexual. She disliked and detested Kyle; he wasn't her type of man. She had always viewed his life-style with distaste, and she could no more imagine the thought of him as her lover than she could...

With a shock of sensation that brought hot colour burning all through her body, she stopped herself. It must be the worry, she thought distractedly, that must be what was causing all these odd thoughts to come to mind.

'Drink?'

It took her several seconds to focus on what he was saying.

'Oh, yes...er...coffee, please...'

'Stay here, I'll go and get it.'

She couldn't help lifting her eyebrows and asking mockingly, 'You'll go and get it? Rather a comedown, isn't it, for the great Kyle Bennett? I should have thought you'd have a string of willing handmaidens to perform such mundane tasks as that.'

'I have a woman from the village who comes in to clean and gets in the shopping for me. You forget, Heather, when you've been institutionalised you soon learn the true value of having your own privacy.'

She felt her skin heat up in shamed embarrassment at her implied lack of insight. It infuriated her that Kyle seemed to have this knack of always putting her in the wrong, of making her feel that her emotional responses were shallow and childish.

As though the small, bitter exchange had never taken place, he asked casually, 'Black or white?'

'White, please.'

When he had gone she stretched out her hands to the fire, luxuriating in its warmth.

'We'll get business out of the way first and then we'll have lunch. I hope you still like chicken casserole.'

'We're eating *here*?'

'Why not? You don't have any objection, do you? I promise you I'm not going to poison you. I've rather a lot to get through before I leave for the States, and, to be honest, I simply don't have the time to drive a dozen or more miles to eat what would probably be an indifferent meal, surrounded by the unedifying babble of the conversation of others.'

'Forgive me, I'm sorry if I'm taking up too much of your valuable time,' Heather interrupted sarcastically, still sore from their previous exchange, and reaching for her bag. '*You* were the one who wanted to talk, Kyle. I...'

'All right, come down off your high horse.'

Heather gasped as he took hold of her and firmly pushed her down into a chair.

'God, why on earth is it that you always have to twist everything I say, Heather? If I hadn't *wanted* to see you today, I wouldn't have suggested that we have lunch together but, having said that, I felt that what we had to say to one another could best be said in the comfort and privacy of my home than over a dining-table in public.'

He had a point, of course, but Heather didn't want to acknowledge it.

'And, of course, my time isn't valuable, is that it?' she demanded acidly. 'It doesn't matter that I've had to waste over an hour driving here, and then an hour driving back, two hours when I could have been working.'

'Could you?' Kyle asked her wryly, reaching down on to the table in front of him and picking up their order book.

As he deliberately thumbed through the betrayingly empty pages, Heather fought to control her chagrin.

'All right, so we don't have a lot of orders on hand at the moment, but . . .'

'But nothing, Heather. The business is finished. You know it and I know it,' he interrupted flatly. 'Your father's heading for bankruptcy unless he gets out now, and I mean *now* . . . like immediately. I've been to see your mother this morning—which is why I invited you *here*, by the way. She's agreed, and so has your father, that I can take over the business with immediate effect. From this morning, your father's company officially became a part of Bennett Enterprises.'

Heather stared at him. 'You've taken over the company? But . . .'

'Lock, stock and barrel,' Kyle told her calmly. 'Between us, your mother and I managed to persuade your father that he's never going to be physically strong enough again to go back on the road and run the business as well. To be honest with you, I think he was quite relieved by my offer. I've paid him enough for the company to ensure that he and your mother will have a comfortable retirement.'

'You've *paid* for the company? You mean, you've *bought* it from him?'

'Is there any other way of acquiring someone else's business legally, other than marrying into it?' Kyle asked sardonically. 'Certainly I've bought it from him. Come on, Heather, you know your father. Did you honestly think he would sit back and simply allow me to pay for his operation?'

Of course, he was right.

'But the company isn't worth anything,' she told him slowly. 'My father knows that...'

'I've managed to convince him otherwise,' Kyle told her coolly, 'And in point of fact it could be worth something to me eventually, if only from the point of view of its excellent reputation.'

'But we're window-dressers...you don't own any shops.'

'Not at the moment, but I am building, or rather developing, a small and very exclusive arcade of boutiques in Bath which will be let out under an umbrella scheme to ensure that anyone who rents one will conform to the very high standards we intend to set. The service we will provide as management could well benefit from the inclusion of a specialist window-dressing service.'

It all sounded so plausible, and yet Heather knew that her father's business was virtually worthless.

'How much did you pay him?' she asked hesitantly, her mouth dry.

Immediately his face closed up against her, his mouth thin and harsh.

'I can't tell you that. It's something between your father and myself.'

Instantly she felt as though a door had been slammed in her face; she felt shut out and rejected, a feeling she was intensely familiar with from her childhood and, as she had done then, she retreated now behind a protective barrier of sarcasm.

'Nothing's changed, has it, Kyle? You still resent me just as much as I resent you. You're just smarter at hiding it, that's all.'

'That's certainly one way of looking at it, I suppose,' he agreed after a long silence. He was looking at her in an odd and unfamiliar way; as though something about her...hurt him...

Shrugging off the thought, Heather glared belligerently at him.

'I'm not going to let you provoke me into a row, Kyle. I can't pretend to see what it is my parents see in you, other than the fact that you're male,' she told him bitterly, unwittingly betraying her own carefully hidden insecurity. 'But for *their* sakes...'

'*Is* that really it?' Kyle asked her softly, not allowing her to finish. 'Is it my masculinity you're envious of, Heather?'

'No!' Her exclamation was an instant and vehement denial of the cynical implication she could read in the bitter twist of his mouth. She was more than happy with her femininity, and the implication behind Kyle's soft words brought a furious scorch of colour to her face.

'No...nothing like that.' She swallowed hard, knowing that she had unwittingly allowed herself to stray on to very dangerous ground.

Kyle was watching her like a cat at a mousehole, and he wasn't going to let her escape without at least a token explanation.

Remembering the advice of her counsellor, she forced herself to swallow down her pride, and to ignore her natural inclination to keep her most intimate and personal thoughts hidden. Instead, she said huskily, 'Once...before you came to live with us, my mother lost a baby. It...he would have been a boy. I once overheard someone talking about it. She...they implied...or at least I interpreted their conversation to mean that my parents considered a daughter very much second-best.'

She waited in horror for him to taunt her with her revelation, but instead he said nothing.

She had delivered her husky, proud admission to the fireplace, not daring to look straight at him, and now as she caught his movement on the periphery of her vision she automatically flinched, as though waiting for a blow.

'I was wrong,' she heard him saying in a harsh voice. 'You have grown up.'

'You don't sound very pleased about it.'

How idiotic to sound so peevish! But she needed to scuttle back into the safety of their normal acid exchanges to be able to cope with the emotional intensity of what had gone before.

'Perhaps I'm not,' he agreed, and then, before she could speak he added quietly, 'Since it seems

to be confession time, I might as well admit that I
resented you as well. It wasn't easy for the child
that I was to accept that your parents loved me
simply for myself. It wasn't something I'd experienced before, you see. You know that my father
deserted my mother—he's dead now, by the way—
and that my mother died. It took me a long time
to accept that your parents loved me for myself and
not because they simply wanted to be seen to be
doing "the right thing" in giving a home to
someone like me.'

'But you walked out and turned your back on
them.'

There was a long silence. She could feel the tense
thud of her heart. They were on the verge of a new
beginning, of a new relationship; so much de-
pended on him being honest with her now.

'I left because I thought I was doing the right
thing for them,' he told her flatly. 'You were their
natural child, it was plain that the two of us could
never live in harmony. After you...after your ac-
cident, I knew it couldn't go on any longer. So I
left...'

'For their sakes?'

He made no response, but Heather knew it was
the truth. It was what she had known all along, and
she felt the tension ease out of her in the knowledge
that he now respected her enough to feel that he
could speak the truth. They could never be close
in a fraternal way, but for the sake of two people
whom they both loved perhaps it would be possible
for them to make a new beginning, Heather
thought, exploring the idea cautiously.

And then he went and spoiled it all by saying carelessly, 'Oh, and if you're worrying about your own job, you needn't. You'll be taking charge of the new Bennett Enterprises window-dressing operation.'

Heather opened her mouth and found that her voice had completely deserted her. When it came, it sounded harsh and hurt her throat. 'I don't want or need your charity, Kyle,' she stormed at him. 'I can find my own job.'

'Can you?' His cynical disbelief hurt her almost as much as it infuriated her.

'I'm fully qualified...I have my degree...'

His mouth was still twisted in that bitterly cynical way that always sparked off her temper, implying as it did that he had a greater and more powerful knowledge of something to which she was excluded.

'I'm not questioning your qualifications, or your skill. But jobs of the type you're qualified for aren't exactly thick on the ground round here, are they? Think about it, Heather, what are you trying to say? That you want to leave here and go and try your luck in London? Perhaps if you're lucky, landing yourself a job as the most junior member of a store window-dressing team, forced to carry out the instructions and ideas of others, always competing with younger and more enthusiastic graduates than yourself.'

The picture he was painting was grim enough to make her close her eyes and shudder. She hated the thought of working and living in London; she always had. She was not ambitious as such, but she loved her work; he was right, she would hate working under someone else's direction. She was used to her father giving her a completely free hand and, if she was honest with herself, she enjoyed the responsibility.

A sudden thought struck her, the words almost sticking in her throat as she demanded huskily, 'This is my father's idea, isn't it? He *made* you offer me this job... he asked you...'

'Think what you like, Heather. I'm not prepared to discuss the whys and wherefores of a job offer with a potential employee. It isn't my normal practice.'

Only just in time she stopped herself from bursting into a furious tirade. She looked suspiciously at him, wondering if he was trying deliberately to goad her into taking a stand.

'I don't want the job,' she told him flatly.

'You don't? You're a very lucky woman to be able to make such a decision,' he marvelled cynically. 'How are you going to support yourself without a job, Heather, or are you going to leave that small matter to your parents?'

And indirectly to him, Heather realised on a sudden mortified flood of realisation. She bit down hard on her bottom lip. Pride had forced her to reject his job offer because she suspected he was simply making a position for her because of her father, and yet if she didn't take it, if she had no job at all...

'Poor Heather... caught up in a no-win situation, aren't you?'

'And how you're enjoying it!' she retaliated sharply, her eyes narrowing as she glared at him.

To her chagrin, he laughed. 'You remind me of a spitting wildcat when you narrow your eyes like that. You look for all the world as though there's nothing you'd like more than to pounce on me and claw the flesh from my throat.'

To her horror, Heather felt a betraying heat spread through her body, not at the violence of his suggestion, but at the sexuality he had so cleverly cloaked beneath it.

She stared at him, nonplussed by her own reaction. His face was unreadable, so unreadable, in fact, that she had trouble in deciding whether or not she had actually heard that sexuality or imagined it.

'If you don't take the job I'll have to find someone else to fill it. From what I've seen of your work, you've got the skills the operation will need.'

He was beginning to sound bored, and Heather caught the indifference edging up under his voice.

'I don't want charity, Kyle,' she told him fiercely.

He looked at her. 'You won't be getting it. Now, do you want the job or not?'

She wavered between refusing it as her pride demanded and a far more commonsense approach. Her parents would be pleased and relieved if she accepted it; they would see it not as just a job, but as a sign that she had finally accepted Kyle.

'I...I want it,' she said huskily, bending her head so that he wouldn't see the defeat in her eyes.

'Good...I'll see that you get an employment contract as soon as I get back from the States.'

It confused her to see him like this, very much in control, and all brisk and businesslike. It was hard to accept that this was the same person she had traded insults with for most of her growing years. The same teenager she had bitten in the leg in a fit of fury because he wouldn't let her ride his bicycle! A rogue smile tugged at the corners of her mouth at that memory.

'Why the smile? Not planning my early demise, I hope?'

She frowned. 'What makes you think that?'

'I don't know...possibly something to do with a painting I once saw of Lucretia Borgia,' Kyle told her drily.

'Well, you're quite wrong. I was just thinking about that time I bit you in the leg because you wouldn't let me ride your bike.'

His eyebrows shot up, and for a moment Heather thought he didn't remember. And then he smiled, and there was something in the mocking smile that turned her insides upside-down.

'Oh, yes...I ought to thank you for that.' He saw her wary expression and laughed. 'You see, it left a scar.' He touched his thigh reflectively. 'Most interestingly positioned, and the cause of much feminine speculation and—er—concern.'

Heather glared at him, hating him for deliberately making her so aware of his sexuality.

'I told them I had been bitten by a rabid dog,' he added reflectively, another smile tugging at his mouth.

'Of the female variety, of course,' Heather responded.

He caught her drift and his eyebrows lifted.

'You're underestimating yourself,' he told her mockingly. 'If I had to compare you to any member of the animal kingdom it would be to a wild she-cat: all claws, snarls and lashing tail.'

His eyes dropped to her hands, and to her consternation Heather discovered, as she followed his gaze downwards, that her fingers were curled as though ready to strike out at her prey.

He laughed, a soft, satisfied sound that made her skin tingle and raised a rash of goose-bumps under it. 'I've often wondered if you've ever fulfilled that promise of passion that was so much a part of those early teenage years.'

'That's something you're never going to know.'

The hoarse intensity of her voice shocked her. What was she doing, allowing him to inveigle her into this kind of confrontation; a type of confrontation she could only retreat from in disorder?

She knew nothing of the sexual pleasure he was hinting at, and as for passion . . . !

'Don't tell me you really prefer your lovers tame and timid, like the poor specimen you had with you the other night? Or was it a case of needs must?'

He showed her his teeth in a savage grin. Her breath seemed to have leaked away somewhere deep inside her chest, and her lungs heaved as she tried desperately to breathe.

What was happening to her? What was he doing to her? Certainly he was showing her a side of himself he had always previously kept discreetly camouflaged. But she had always known it was there, had always known that he was an intensely sensual human being. How had she known that? She shivered again, tormented by the shocking intimacy of her thoughts.

A thousand excuses for her immediate departure clamoured for utterance, but to give voice to them would be cowardly, and more, it would betray to him just how disturbing she found their conversation. She had to play him at his own game, to show him how adult she was. He was just trying to get under her skin, he was tormenting her as he had tormented her so often in the past, but now he was using far more sophisticated weapons. He couldn't know that her total sexual experience was limited to a few fumbled caresses and unedifying kisses. He couldn't know how weak and shivery he made her feel, just by talking to her the way he was.

'I think it's time we had lunch.'

The abrupt return to normality overwhelmed her. She suspected that he was doing everything he could to keep her on edge, and she was determined that she wouldn't let him see that he had got through to her. She had always known how clever he was; how cunning and determined to have his own way. He might profess to want a better relationship between them, but she was under no illusions; deep down inside, he still resented her, just as she still resented him.

All right, in her case that resentment was tinged with guilt and touched by a compassion she could not help feeling for the child he had once been, rejected and unloved. She was mature enough, yes, and woman enough to feel that, but he still made her feel as prickly and defensive as a threatened animal; he still made her walk warily and watch carefully.

'Everything's ready. We'll be eating in the dining-room. It's this way.'

The dining-room was furnished with the same simplicity as the rooms Heather had already seen, very much in keeping with the age of the house, the dark-panelled walls glistening softly in the firelight.

'You realise, don't you, that there are going to have to be some changes?' Kyle told her abruptly, once he had served their meal.

She should not have been surprised at his skill, her mother had, after all, insisted on teaching both of them how to look after themselves, just as her father had taught them both to drive and to carry out small household maintenance tasks. There was no sexual bigotry in her parents' household, apart, of course, from the fact that they had always wanted a son.

She put down her knife and fork, ignoring the delicious chicken casserole, her thoughts winging back to the past.

'Heather, did you hear me?'

She frowned and looked down the length of the polished oak table.

'Yes, you said something about things changing.'

'Mmm...the house, for instance. After his operation, those stairs will be too much for your father. Your mother was talking about buying a small villa in Portugal. Apparently they've always liked the country. Then they could spend their winters there...'

He was going too fast for her, covering ground she had not even yet had time to consider. She knew what he said was correct, but the thought of losing the house that had been home to her for so long, the thought of her parents actually taking the decision to sell...

'With a bit of luck, your father should be out of hospital before Christmas, and then he and your mother will fly straight to my villa in Portugal and stay there until he's fully recovered. Have you made any plans for Christmas?' he asked her, apparently unaware of her sudden lack of appetite, as he ate his own meal with gusto.

Christmas! She had not even got as far as thinking about how she would spend it. Normally, it was a big event, with her parents' friends descending on the house. Her mother loved it, and so had her father. But this year...

'A few,' she lied carelessly, not wanting him to know that, with her parents away, her Christmas would be very bleak indeed. She didn't want him to accuse her of being selfish again, of putting her own feelings before those of her mother and father.

'A pity. You'll have to cancel them.'

'Cancel?' Heather stared at him. 'What are you talking about?'

'I've promised your parents that I'll make sure that you spend Christmas here with me. Apparently they're concerned about you staying in the house on your own, and I must say I can see why.'

'For goodness' sake, I'm twenty-three years old, and perfectly capable of taking care of myself! I'm not likely to try and commit suicide just because I'm spending Christmas alone,' she threw at him bitterly.

'No one suggested that you might, but that house *is* rather remote, and your father says the central heating's on the blink. He's also concerned about the van. He says it isn't very reliable or safe. OK, so you and I know you'd be perfectly safe and certainly much happier on your own than you're likely to be here, but for their sake can I suggest that you give in quietly?'

'Is that what you did?'

The silence stretched for too long for her to deceive herself that she was wrong. Kyle wanted her staying with him as little as she wanted to be there.

'All right,' she gave in wearily. 'And I promise I'll do my best to keep out of your way...'

'I'll give you a spare key before you go. You could move your stuff in while I'm away in the States. There's a guest suite upstairs, you can use that. When I get back I'll show you the plans for the new shopping arcade, and you can tell me what you think.'

He tossed the comment to her as casually as an adult throwing a child a sweet, and without her being aware of it her eyes flashed dangerously.

'All that wasted passion,' he mocked her. 'There's only one way you're ever going to get to dig those sharp claws of yours into my skin, and it's not by losing your temper with me.' He laughed at her flushed, shocked face. 'Perish the thought, eh?' he taunted softly. 'Don't worry. I doubt I'll ever be that desperate.'

'It wouldn't matter if you were,' Heather retaliated when she had got her breath back. 'There's no way I'd ever let you...'

'Take you to bed? Don't tempt fate,' he advised her, and for a moment she was almost tempted to believe that he was actually contemplating what he was threatening, and then she remembered that he had always had a Machiavellian sense of humour, and decided instantly that if he thought he was going to get to exercise it now at her expense he could think again.

'Why not?' she retorted carelessly, giving a dazzling and very manufactured smile. 'I doubt that even you could teach me anything I don't already know. I'm not seventeen any more now, Kyle. A macho display of sexuality is hardly likely to send me into a flutter of confusion these days.'

'So it seems, but just let's get one thing clear, shall we? In private, I'm prepared to take just as many insults as you care to dish out, but in public...'

'Your image is *that* fragile?' She smiled with sweet malice.

'No, but your father's health is,' he reminded her brutally. 'And, for his sake, I suggest that you at least try to pretend you can be in my company for over five minutes without wanting to shred the skin from my back.'

Heather stood up, shrugging. 'That's fine by me, but I don't like being goaded, Kyle. Kick me and I kick back.'

'Does the same thing apply in reverse? Are you as responsive to kisses as you are to "kicks" I wonder?'

'That's...' They were back where they had started, and she checked the words, holding them back. Instead, she said acidly, 'That's for me to know...'

'And me to find out?' Kyle murmured suggestively. 'Well, well. I never thought that...'

'No, that's not what I meant,' Heather protested, flustered. 'You know it wasn't. Oh, for heaven's sake!' she groaned, capitulating. 'Will you please stop confusing me with all this innuendo? All right, maybe we can never be true friends, but surely we can do better than this?'

The plea came from her heart, her defences going down as she realised how ill equipped she was to deal with a man of his calibre.

'Please, Kyle, help me,' she pleaded despairingly. 'You're right, it will hurt my parents dreadfully if they see us quarrelling, but all this is new territory for me.'

She held her breath, dreading hearing him make the kind of sardonic response that would show that he was not taking her plea seriously, or, worse, that he was amused.

His reply was a long time in coming and when it did, it made her body tense with shock, and yes, pleasure, too, she recognised later, when she tried to analyse the multiplicity of sensations she had experienced.

'I take back *all* the insulting things I ever said about you,' he told her quietly. 'You've grown up to become one hell of a woman, Heather: female enough to resent being verbally attacked, and yet big enough to put aside those feelings and lower your defences. I don't know if you scare me the most when you look at me as though you'd like to see me burst into flames in front of your eyes, or when you look at me the way you're doing right now. Friends?' He shook his head and said softly, 'No, maybe we'll never be that, but for what it's worth you have my respect.'

It was worth more than she could ever tell him; with those few words he had wiped out a raw wound so old and so deep that she had forgotten it was

there. It was only the sudden cessation of its ache
that reminded her. Ever since the folly of her attempted suicide, part of her had despised herself
for her weakness, for using such cruel emotional
blackmail on those who had loved her. She had lost
her own self-respect, and for Kyle to say that she
had his was like being given back a part of herself.
She felt a tremendous inner softening toward him,
an urge to go up to him and touch him, a need to
almost physically embrace him, as though they were
indeed brother and sister. But as she reached for
him he side-stepped, widening the gap between
them, his face suddenly taut and harsh.

'Let's just leave it there, shall we? You'd better
start making tracks, that sky doesn't look too
promising.'

He had rejected her, had rejected her physical
overture of... of regret and affection, and she felt
so cold inside that her muscles ached and hurt the
way her flesh did when she was physically cold.

It was on her mind all the way home. *Why* had
he done that to her? Why had he almost pushed
her off, as though he loathed the very idea of her
touch?

Why not? part of herself argued hardily. Up until
that particular moment in time, if asked, she would
have said that *she* loathed the thought of being
touched by him.

They could have shared so much, if only she
hadn't been so determined to shut him out of her
life. They could have... but it was pointless
mourning now the brother he could have been. It
was too late to turn back the clock. She could only
go on, and hope that one day she would break

through the barrier he had thrown up between them and convince him that . . .

That what? Heather didn't know. She only knew that she was conscious of a tremendous loss; of a great sadness and heaviness of heart; of a sensation of having stupidly deprived herself of something she would mourn for the rest of her life.

CHAPTER FIVE

THAT sensation of almost being at one with Kyle didn't last very long.

The snow was still holding off, although the late afternoon sky was ominously heavy with its winter burden. On impulse, instead of spending the day working as she had intended to do, Heather turned the van round and drove into Bristol. Once there, she was lucky enough to be able to park it relatively close to the shops.

Seeing families battling through the busy streets, their arms piled high with brightly coloured packages, made her realise how close Christmas was—something she had forgotten in the aftermath of her father's collapse, when all her energies had been concentrated on willing him to get better.

This would be the first Christmas she had not spent with her parents. She could see the wisdom of Kyle's insistence that they go away to Portugal just as soon as her father was fit enough to travel. Several weeks spent snowed up in a cold, draughty house worrying about heating bills was hardly likely to aid his recuperation, while a month or two spent in what she was sure would be luxurious sur-roundings, in Kyle's Portuguese villa . . .

She was being selfish to wish that Kyle had sug-gested that she should go with them. He had made it clear to her that the job he was offering her was no manufactured sinecure and, that being the case,

she had no right to expect to be allowed to take
time off in order to spend the best part of the winter
with her parents. And yet it hurt that Kyle had not
even suggested that she might fly over to Portugal
just to spend Christmas with them.

What on earth would the pair of them find to
say to one another, cooped up in that beautiful
house of his? Would they manage to last out the
Christmas season without quarreling? Kyle obviously wanted her there as little as she wanted to
be there. No doubt normally he spent his Christmas
somewhere exotic, like the Caribbean, or perhaps
somewhere more traditional, but just as expensive,
such as Gstaad. And of course, whichever location
he chose, no doubt there would be a beautiful
woman to accompany him, to...

Abruptly, she stopped still in the street. What
was it about Kyle that sparked off this almost un-
controllable surge of physical awareness? Even his
conversation had been sprinkled with acidly barbed
sexual innuendo. She shivered tensely, digging her
hands deep into the pockets of her old coat. What
was it that had changed so much between them and
that made her so intensely aware of Kyle as a man?

The resentment, the dislike, the antagonism;
these were all emotions she remembered and
understood; but this new sexual undercurrent, this
alien and dangerously strong power that moved
through her whenever she was with him, this was
new. Completely new, she admitted, oblivious to
the curious stares of passers by at her motionless
figure. This was something she had never experienced before in her life. And she didn't want to
experience it now.

Slowly, almost painfully, she started to move, all her concentration turned inwards as she forced herself to confront the warring anomalies within her own personality.

Why was it she should react so strongly to Kyle, when all the other men she knew left her completely cold?

It wasn't a question she could answer and, because it made her feel so uncomfortable and almost alienated from herself, she pushed it to the back of her mind, and concentrated instead on looking for the small Christmas presents she had come to Bristol to buy.

Christmas was normally one of her favourite times of the year. On Christmas Eve she loved to walk into the shabby sitting-room and see the presents piled up under the tree.

At eleven they always left for Midnight Mass, and then afterwards had friends back for some of her mother's home-made wine and mince pies. Despite the fact that they went to bed late, they were always up early in the morning to unwrap their presents and get ready for the almost constant onslaught of visitors who called throughout the day.

This year there would be none of that to look forward to. Her hand tensed on the small box of scented soaps she had been examining. What was she going to do with herself, cooped up with Kyle for the whole of the Christmas holidays?

Her eye was caught by a display of books, and she grimaced faintly. She would have to stock up with plenty of good reading; that would help to pass the time.

If she was Kyle, she wouldn't welcome her stay at all, she recognised, wondering uncomfortably what plans he might have made that her presence would spoil.

It was ridiculous of her parents to expect him to take her in! Good heavens, she wasn't a *child*; she was perfectly capable of looking after herself.

Disconsolately she put the box down, unaware of the frowning irritation of the girl behind the counter.

She couldn't get out of going, and it would be childish to try. Surely she was capable of enduring less than a week of Kyle's company, for the sake of her parents' peace of mind? It was no use telling herself that she was an adult; in their eyes, she was still vulnerable, and she admitted that she would hate her father's recovery to be held up by any action of hers.

Moving more briskly, she headed for another shop. It was silly to waste time worrying about how she would cope with Kyle when she had so much to do. She looked down at the list in her hand, and frowned slightly over her own handwriting.

Normally they all did this together, taking more pleasure in buying their small gifts than most other people seemed to do in spending much greater sums.

Another book caught her eye. It was one she knew her parents would love and she bought it on impulse, even though it was expensive. She only hoped that there would be enough space left in their cases for it.

Although her mother was able to visit the hospital whenever she wished, Heather tried to keep to normal visiting hours, so as not to disrupt the ward too much. A glance at her watch reminded her that it was time for her to go if she wanted to see her father.

The hospital was within pleasant walking distance, and chill winds made her hurry along briskly.

Nurses hurried in and out of the building like busy worker bees, an ambulance pulling to a screaming halt as Heather approached. Averting her head, she quelled the sick despair flooding through her body at the sound of its siren. Since her father's collapse she had nightmares about hearing that ominous sound.

The ward was a long one, with her father in a smaller four-bedded room at one end.

As she pushed the door, Heather heard voices, and tensed, recognising Kyle's.

'She seems to...'

Abruptly he broke off and turned his head.

An unwelcome sense of *déjà vu* engulfed Heather as she stood there, but she knew well from where the unwanted memory came. It was her childhood all over again. A childhood during which she had felt that she stood on the outside, while her parents and Kyle formed a small, exclusive adult group that excluded her.

Her immediate impulse was to turn and run, as she had done many times as a child, but she managed to quell it, and instead forced her lips to curve into some semblance of a smile.

Her father, she saw now, was watching her with loving, concerned eyes, and she focused her attention on him, ignoring Kyle's tall, dark figure at his bedside.

'You didn't say you were coming to visit Dad.' She couldn't do a thing to stop herself from making the small, stinging remark, and however much she wished it unsaid when she saw her mother's quick concerned frown, the best she could do was to add quickly, 'If I'd known, I'd have begged a ride with you. The van isn't too reliable at the moment.'

'It was an impulse decision,' Kyle said smoothly, but she could read the condemnation in his eyes and knew that he could see through her smile to the bitterness in her heart.

'Kyle's just been telling us that you'll be staying with him over Christmas. I must say that it will be a relief to know that you'll be with him.'

'It's very kind of him to have me.' What else could she say? 'I must say I rather envy you two, though, sunning yourself in Portugal while we'll probably be knee-deep in snow.'

'Well, I have to admit I am looking forward to it,' her mother responded, adding with a quick look at her husband, 'Of course, it all depends on how well your father responds to the surgery. I was going to ring you tonight. The specialist has been to see him already.' The warm smile she gave Kyle made Heather clench her teeth to stop the sharp, bitter protest leaving her throat. 'Kyle's been absolutely marvellous, taking all the worry off our shoulders. The specialist has scheduled the operation for the day after tomorrow.'

Kyle frowned. 'I wish I could put off this trip to the States, but I'm afraid it's impossible. I should be back in a couple of days, though. Heather, perhaps you could pick me up at the airport? I'll get a taxi out there, but they aren't always easy to come by when you land. I'll leave a set of keys for the Jaguar. It is insured...'

Heather wanted to protest that she had no intention of driving his car, nor of picking him up, but just in time she remembered why she had embarked on this venture in the first place, and said dulcetly instead, 'I'll try to make sure I'm there on time.'

She saw Kyle look at his watch.

'I'd better go.'

He turned to kiss her mother, and automatically Heather stepped back from him. She saw that he had not missed the significance of her withdrawal when he looked grimly at her, but he said nothing, turning instead to her father.

'I'll see you when I get back.'

The comparison between her father, so tired and grey in his hospital bed, and Kyle, so full of vitality and health, tore at Heather's heart. She had to turn away to hide the sudden shimmer of tears filming her eyes. She hated anyone to see her cry, and Kyle most of all.

'Remember,' he told her quietly, as he turned to leave, 'I expect to find you installed in the house when I come back.'

'I can't tell you what it's meant to us to see Kyle again,' her mother said quietly once he had gone. 'It's done your father so much good, and the fact that he's insisting on buying the company has lifted such a weight from our shoulders. He says he's told you all about his plans.'

Surely that wasn't a touch of wariness in her mother's voice? It hurt just to think that her parents might be apprehensive of her reaction to Kyle's takeover.

'Yes, yes, he has, and I think Dad's done the best thing,' Heather said firmly. 'I must say that I'm looking forward to starting my new job.'

She managed to sound so enthusiastic that she even surprised herself, but it was worth the deceit to see the smile of relief in her mother's eyes, as her whole expression lightened.

'Oh, darling, I'm pleased for you. You were wasting your talents with the company. This job with Kyle will open up a whole new way of life for you. Are you excited about the New Year's Eve "do"? From what Kyle was telling me about it, it promises to be a fabulous event.' Heather frowned, and her mother checked herself, and bit her lip. 'Oh dear, he hasn't told you, has he? He must have wanted to keep it as a surprise.'

More likely, Kyle hadn't told her because he knew quite well that she would refuse to join in with his plans, Heather thought angrily.

'Come on, Mum, you might as well tell me now,' she insisted, trying to look excited and pleased.

'Well, promise me you'll try and look surprised when Kyle tells you?'

'Yes...yes, of course. Now, don't keep me in suspense any longer. What "do"?'

'Well, it seems that Kyle has been invited to a very grand masked ball to be held at a private house just outside Bath on New Year's Eve. It's something to do with the fact that his firm did most of the restoration work on it. Anyway, everyone has to wear period costume, and Kyle said that in view of the fact that his house was built in the

Elizabethan era he thought he would hire a costume
of that age. He asked me for your measurements
so that he could hire a costume for you...'

Heather fought back the jolt of anger that burned
deep inside her. Her mother looked as pleased and
excited as a small child. How could Heather explain to her how angry and resentful she felt at
Kyle's high-handed action? Where she saw his be-
havior as superior and interfering, her mother
plainly saw it as generous and thoughtful.

Kyle Bennett was someone they would never see
eye to eye on, and for the sake of her parents' peace
of mind she would just have to pretend that she
thought he was as wonderful as they did.

'Promise me that you won't let him guess that
you know,' her mother begged. 'I think he wants
it all to be a surprise for you.'

'I shan't say a word,' Heather assured her, mentally deciding that there was no way Kyle was going
to force her into going with him. No way at all.
'I'm surprised that Kyle isn't going away for
Christmas,' she remarked casually, changing the
subject. 'It seems rather dull for such an eligible
and wealthy bachelor to stay at home. Unless, of
course, he's having guests.'

'Not as far as I know.' Her mother responded
innocently to Heather's probing. 'He did say that
as this was the first year he's owned the house, he
wanted to spend Christmas in it. Is it as lovely as
it sounds?'

'Yes,' Heather admitted rather shortly. In fact,
although she wasn't going to say so, the house came
so close to the sort of home she had always dreamed

of owning herself that it was hard not to feel envious of Kyle for owning it.

'Kyle did mention that he was anxious to do justice to it with his Christmas decorations,' her mother continued uncertainly. 'I did suggest that you might be able to give him a hand?'

It was plain from her expression that she was faintly apprehensive of Heather's reaction.

It hurt to discover that her parents still thought that she had to be treated like spun glass, that they still felt they had to walk on tiptoe around her in some instances.

'It's the least I can do to repay him for putting me up,' Heather responded evenly. 'In fact, the house is so lovely that decorating it for Christmas will be much more of a pleasure than a chore. It's hard to believe that it's less than a month away.'

'I know...the specialist was saying that once he's sure the operation's a success your father can leave for Portugal almost straight away. Kyle's already checked, and apparently there's a first-rate American hospital not far from the villa and he's already arranged all your father's aftercare.'

It was all wrong that she should feel this helplessness, this feeling that time was rolling back and that she was once again tongue-tied and resentful in the face of her parents' obvious love for a boy she could only hate.

This time, it wasn't going to be like that. Kyle could never usurp her own place in her parents' hearts, nor did he want to.

As she held hard to that thought, mercifully Heather felt the red mist of mingled pain and misery fade. Shakily she drew in one breath and then another, a dizzy, giddy feeling of release.

Pleasure filled her and she felt so light with it that she could almost have floated up to the ceiling. It worked; she had used her own will-power, her adult conception of the past and present, her own self-control to beat back the demons of her childhood, and she had won. It wasn't Kyle who was her enemy, she recognised, but her own deep-rooted insecurity.

Her counsellor had told her that years ago, and she had accepted his word, but there was a vast difference in being told where the problem lay and in accepting and knowing it for oneself.

'You look as though someone's just given you the stars,' her father commented.

'Nothing so mundane,' she teased him with a grin, refusing to be drawn, despite his curious questioning. And then, because she could see her father was getting tired, and because a part of her wanted to be alone so that she could savour her first true victory over the misery of her insecurity, she bent and kissed him swiftly and then turned to her mother.

'It's time I left. I've still got some shopping to do, and I don't want to leave it too late. The sky looked very ominous this afternoon.'

'I don't like the thought of you driving that van in bad weather conditions,' her father fretted, frowning.

'I'll be perfectly all right. You know how careful I am,' she soothed him.

'Ring us when you get back,' her mother suggested quietly. 'That will put your father's mind at rest.'

It was only later, as she drove back through the darkness, that she realised that for a girl of her age she was, perhaps, a little too close to her parents, a little too cherished and protected.

Now where had that idea come from? Did she really need to ask herself? Kyle, of course; that look of his, that suggested that she was wrapped up in protective cotton wool, safe from the realities of life and its pains, had found its mark.

Was it her fault if she preferred country pursuits and a country life-style? Was it her fault that she lived at home and enjoyed living there? Was it her fault that she was not by nature independent? And yet, hadn't there been more and more occasions over the last couple of years when she had chafed, if only momentarily, at her parents' loving concern?

A frown touched her forehead as she remembered one of her dates challenging her to deny that she lived with and worked for her parents because she was frightened of the risks of going it alone.

Was she? Her chin tilted proudly. No, she wasn't. In fact, already a tiny part of her was actively looking forward to the challenge of working for Kyle. If she was honest with herself, the job he was offering her was exactly the sort of thing she had always dreamed of doing. He would be exhaustingly demanding to work for, his standards almost impossibly high; she knew that, and yet he was offering her an opportunity to show what she could really do, given the chance.

If only this awareness of him as a man wasn't there to disturb her hard-won maturity. She shivered, and then braked to avoid a cyclist, her concentration switching back to her driving.

On impulse, the day before her father's operation, the day when she should have been packing her bags ready to move them into Kyle's guest suite, she got on a train for London instead, and spent the best part of the day wandering around the capital's more exclusive shopping venues, her artist's eye noting the wealth of detail.

Travelling home, she ached to get down to work; already she was imagining just what she would be able to achieve given a sensible budget and a free hand.

There was a nostalgia for the past that was evident in shops as diverse as Laura Ashley through to the very up-market Ralph Lauren. Bath, with its elegant Georgian terraces, Nash terraces and Georgian squares, was almost custom-made for a haunting echo of other eras, in a way that Heather was determined would have nothing about it that was remotely chocolate-boxy, or overdone.

No, her nostalgia would be discreet and subtle.

Full of ideas, she dug deep into her bag for her notebook and pen and started to scribble.

She'd worked all day without a break, and now already it was growing dark.

A cold, silent house greeted her. Meg was being looked after for the day by a neighbour and the cats were fast asleep. Heather realised the moment she walked in that the temperamental heating boiler had gone into a terminal sulk.

Half an hour later, ready to concede defeat, she shivered in the coldness of the empty house. Outside, the first fine flakes of snow were starting to fall. The long threatened snow had arrived.

Having rung the hospital and checked on her father, she put down the phone and sighed. Her mother had been concerned that she wasn't already installed at Kyle's.

Staying in an empty cold house had less and less appeal, and besides, there were so many ideas she wanted to discuss with Kyle. It was amazing how easy it was to push aside her past dislike and resentment once she had accepted that they sprang from within her own personality and, once or twice, as she hurried with her packing, she was amazed to discover a sensation bubbling up inside her that was almost akin to excited anticipation.

The very last thing she did was to pop the cats into their travelling boxes, and then go round the house, checking that all was secure.

She was picking Meg up on the way, and only hoped that Kyle knew what he was letting himself in for in opening his home to the four of them.

Her neighbour insisted on making her a cup of tea, and of course she wanted to know all about the state of her father's health, in addition to expressing a very natural curiosity as to where Heather herself was going to stay.

At length, Heather got up to go. Meg, who loved travelling, couldn't wait to jump into the van, and the four of them set off.

She felt rather like a character from an Edward Lear poem, Heather reflected, as the headlights of the van picked out the winding ribbon of road, now whitened by the still falling snow. She had decided to use the quiet back roads into and out of Bath, all too conscious of the van's rather shaky physical state, and not wanting to risk the danger of the motorway with its high-powered and sometimes reckless drivers. Common sense and necessity both made her keep her speed down, and she had no desire to have some impatient and foolhardy driver sitting on her tail, desperate to get past her.

She kept the radio on to check on the weather bulletins, eyeing the thickening flakes of snow with unease. The van hated cold weather at the best of times, and she just prayed it would get her to Kyle's home without breaking down.

She was unlucky. Less than ten miles from Kyle's house, the van's engine coughed, spluttered and then abruptly died.

Cursing under her breath, Heather tried to re-start it, but the dull, ominous whine it gave warned her that her task was hopeless.

She had no idea where she was; the countryside was pitch-black, even the stars and moon obscured by the low cloud. She was on a back road, and the chances of being able to flag down another motorist were extremely slim, not to mention potentially dangerous.

Slipping on Meg's lead, she patted the cats' box, and said quietly to the dog, 'You and I are going to have to find ourselves a garage, Meg, old girl. I think we're fairly close to a village...let's hope that I'm not wrong.'

Once outside the van, she shivered beneath the icy sting of the wind. It was colder than she had thought, the snowflakes stinging her exposed face and hands. Meg whined and made to get back in the van, but Heather tugged gently on the lead. She didn't relish the thought of her lonely dark walk, and Meg would be company, as well as a deterrent to...well...anything.

She had walked less than a hundred yards when she heard a vehicle coming towards her. Meg froze, trapped in the headlights of a mud-splattered Land Rover, which rattled to an abrupt stop.

'Hello...having problems?' a cheerful male voice called out. Before Heather could urge Meg away, the driver of the vehicle was climbing out and coming towards her.

She eyed him warily, relieved to discover that he looked quite normal and harmless. He was about her own age, with untidy fair hair, his face weathered and drawn into a grimace against the driving snow. He was only a couple of inches taller than her, and wearing well-padded winter clothes.

He looked like a farmer, Heather thought, pleased to have her guess confirmed when he added, 'I've just been dropping off some fodder for the sheep, and I saw your headlights.'

'My van's broken down...I'm not sure what's wrong...'

'Umm...going far, are you?'

'Marston Old Hall.'

'Kyle Bennett's place?' His interest sharpened. 'He's away at the moment.'

'Yes, I know,' Heather agreed coolly. 'If you could direct me to the nearest garage?'

'There's only one, and it will be closed at this time of night. Known Kyle long, have you?' he asked curiously.

'Most of my life,' Heather told him, her tawny eyes letting him know that she resented his questioning.

Immediately his expression changed. 'Oh, you'll be the daughter of the couple who fostered him, then.'

Heather looked at him suspiciously. What had Kyle told him about her and her parents, and his life with them?

'Mrs Evans, who works for Kyle, mentioned you to my mother. I own Heybridge Farm. We're his nearest neighbours. My mother has her own small business—dairy produce mostly—and, since Mrs Evans is away at the moment, Ma went round this morning to the house with a box of groceries. She tries to mother Kyle a bit, but he's not the type really, is he? When you first mentioned him I thought...'

He coloured and Heather was surprised by her own frisson of awareness. Surely she didn't look as though she might be one of Kyle's women friends? To judge from the photographs she had occasionally seen in the Press, he normally went for glamour types, not untidy, inelegant creatures such as herself.

Her hand went up defensively to push her hair off her face and, as she did, she heard her companion saying boyishly, 'Can't say that I'm not pleased...that you're not...'

'One of Kyle's women?' Heather supplied for him.

'We don't get very many pretty, unattached women round here. Too remote...most of the ones who don't marry virtually straight after school go

WOW!

THE MOST GENEROUS
FREE OFFER EVER!
From the Harlequin Reader Service®

GET 4 FREE BOOKS WORTH $10.00

Affix peel-off stickers to reply card

FOUR FREE BOOKS

FOUR FREE BOOKS

PLUS A FREE VICTORIAN PICTURE FRAME

AND A FREE MYSTERY GIFT!

NO COST! NO OBLIGATION TO BUY!
NO PURCHASE NECESSARY!

Because you're a reader of Harlequin romances, the publishers would like you to accept four brand-new Harlequin Presents® novels, with their compliments. Accepting this offer places you under no obligation to purchase any books, ever!

ACCEPT FOUR BRAND-NEW

YOURS

We'd like to send you four free Harlequin novels, worth $10.00, to introduce you to the benefits of the Harlequin Reader Service®. We hope your free books will convince you to subscribe, but that's up to you. Accepting them places you under no obligation to buy anything, but we hope you'll want to continue your membership in the Reader Service.

So unless we hear from you, once a month we'll send you 6 additional Harlequin Presents® novels to read and enjoy. If you choose to keep them, you'll pay just $2.24* per volume— a saving of 26¢ off the cover price. There is no charge for shipping and handling. There are no hidden extras! And you may cancel at anytime, for any reason, just by sending us a note or a shipping statement marked "cancel." You can even return any shipment to us at our expense. Either way, the free books and gifts are yours to keep!

ALSO FREE!
VICTORIAN PICTURE FRAME

This lovely Victorian pewter-finish miniature is perfect for displaying a treasured photograph—and it's yours *absolutely free*—when you accept our no-risk offer.

Perfect for a treasured Photograph

Plus a FREE mystery Gift —follow instruction at right.

*Terms and prices subject to change without notice.
Sales taxes applicable in NY.

© 1990 Harlequin Enterprises Limite

HARLEQUIN PRESENTS® NOVELS

FREE!

Harlequin Reader Service®

```
┌─────────────────────────────┐
│                             │
│         AFFIX               │
│    FOUR FREE BOOKS          │
│      STICKER HERE           │
│                             │
└─────────────────────────────┘
```

YES, send me my four free books and gifts as explained on the opposite page. I have affixed my "free books" sticker above and my two "free gift" stickers below. I understand that accepting these books and gifts places me under no obligation ever to buy any books; I may cancel at anytime, for any reason, and the free books and gifts will be mine to keep!

106 CIH BA6K
(U-H-P-11/90)

NAME _____
(PLEASE PRINT)

ADDRESS _____ APT. _____

CITY _____

STATE _____ ZIP _____

Offer limited to one per household and not valid to current Harlequin Presents® subscribers. All orders subject to approval.

```
┌───────────────────┐   ┌───────────────────┐
│   AFFIX FREE      │   │                   │
│   VICTORIAN       │   │   AFFIX FREE      │
│   PICTURE         │   │   MYSTERY GIFT    │
│   FRAME           │   │   STICKER HERE    │
│   STICKER HERE    │   │                   │
└───────────────────┘   └───────────────────┘
```

PRINTED IN U.S.A.

WE EVEN PROVIDE FREE POSTAGE!

It costs you *nothing* to send for your free books — we've paid the postage on the attached reply card. And we'll pick up the postage on your shipment of free books and gifts, and also on any subsequent shipments of books, should you choose to become a subscriber. Unlike many book clubs, we charge *nothing* for postage and handling!

DETACH AND RETURN TODAY

BUSINESS REPLY MAIL
FIRST CLASS MAIL   PERMIT NO. 717   BUFFALO, NY

POSTAGE WILL BE PAID BY ADDRESSEE

HARLEQUIN READER SERVICE
PO BOX 1867
BUFFALO NY 14240-9952

NO POSTAGE
NECESSARY
IF MAILED
IN THE
UNITED STATES

off to London or Bath to work and we don't see much of them after that. I can give you a tow to Kyle's place, if you like.'

When Heather agreed, he fixed a tow-rope to her van in a very businesslike manner. His hands were broad, with stubby, capable fingers, reddened by the wind and snow. He caught her watching him and smiled at her, and Heather recognised in his smile his appreciation of her as a woman. She smiled back, flattered by his obvious interest in her.

'There, that should do it.' He gave the knot a testing tug and then walked back to the van with her, checking that she knew how to steer correctly.

His hand touched hers momentarily. The back was covered in fine blond hairs, and she had a momentary memory of Kyle's hands, lean and hard, with long fingers, quick, clever hands, hands that echoed the nature of the man. Hands that it would be dangerous to trust too readily.

'Are you OK?'

Forcing a smile, she nodded.

It didn't take long for David Hartley, as he had introduced himself, to tow her to Kyle's house, but the fact that the snow was thickening to something approaching a blizzard, combined with her realisation that they were the only vehicles using the road, showed her how dangerous her situation had been.

She was sorely tempted to ask him into the house for a cup of coffee, but she was very conscious of the fact that it wasn't her home. He solved her dilemma for her by saying cheerfully that he couldn't stop because his mother would be expecting him in for his evening meal.

'I'll tell her that you've arrived, and no doubt she'll be down to see you in the morning. If you need anything, give us a ring, we're in the phone book.'

He drove off with a cheery wave, having assured himself that she was able to let herself in.

The house was in darkness, but lovely and warm. Meg and the cats soon made themselves at home in the small space off the kitchen, which was obviously used as a store for coats and wellingtons.

Ignoring the rest of the rooms, Heather went upstairs to find the guest suite.

The door had been left open for her, and a fire was laid ready in the grate. She smiled a little wryly at the luxury of an open fire in a bedroom that already had central heating, but appreciated the thoughtfulness of the gesture, nevertheless.

Making her way back to the kitchen, Heather discovered that the fridge was bulging with food. Noting the wrapped cheese and the bowl of eggs, she guessed that the food had been left by David's mother.

An omelette would do her for tonight. Already her stomach was full of nervous butterflies in anticipation of her father's operation. Tonight she would say a special prayer for his safety and his recovery. And, her conscience prodded her, perhaps she ought to say one for Kyle, too, whose generosity had made the operation possible. There had been no mistaking the relief in her father's voice when he'd talked about the business and how pleased he was that Kyle was taking it over. His only concern had been for her, and her reaction to Kyle's job offer.

She would walk Meg, and then she would have an early night. Not that she was expecting to get much sleep—her father's operation was scheduled for early in the morning and would take up the major part of the day. Once it was over, though, he should start to make rapid progress, or so the specialist had said. She could only pray that he was right. If anything should happen to her father... Suddenly and inexplicably, she longed for Kyle to be there with her. She needed his strength to lean on, she admitted, surprised by the discovery. The phone rang on the wall beside her, and she lifted the receiver hesitantly.

'Heather?'

She gave a small start.

'Kyle. Where... where are you?'

He sounded so close that he might almost have been in the next room. She heard him laugh.

'New York. But I should be back some time tomorrow evening. How's your father?'

'Apprehensive, but determined to go through with it.'

'Good... I spoke to your mother earlier. She knows that they're doing the right thing, but naturally she's worried. I only wish I could be there with you...'

'So do I.'

Was that really her saying that? Kyle must have been surprised, too, because she caught his indrawn breath and startled silence.

'You almost sounded as though you meant that '

How well she recognised the mocking derision in his voice, but for once she was too tired, too worried to respond to it in kind.

'I do,' she told him honestly, her voice low and pained.

There was another silence and then he said mockingly, 'Can this really be the Heather I know and love, actually *wanting* my company? What's happened? Caught you at a weak moment, have I?'

His mockery jolted her back to reality. She almost slammed the receiver down on him, and then caught herself in time. The tears that had been threatening cleared as though by magic, her tiredness falling away, her voice suddenly crisp and acid as she responded in kind. 'You must have done, but it's gone now.'

'So you don't want me to fly home on the next available flight to hold your hand, after all?'

His voice was still mocking, but there seemed to be an odd degree of seriousness behind the mockery. Dismissing it, Heather said flippantly, 'No way!' And then for good measure, she added, 'Actually, if I need any hand-holding done, you seem to have a neighbour who'd be quite happy to oblige.'

Heaven alone knew what made her make that silly little boast, however true it might be. There was silence from Kyle's end of the line, and then when he spoke his voice sounded distant and cold.

'I take it you mean David Hartley?' he demanded, his voice hardening.

'Yes, we met when ... by chance,' she amended hastily, not wanting to admit the demise of the van or the lateness of her arrival.

'Don't be deceived by that mock-naïve farmer's boy air, Heather,' Kyle told her curtly. 'David Hartley is already responsible for the arrival of one illegitimate child, and I dare say he wouldn't be averse to fathering another, not if local gossip is anything to go by.'

All the breath hissed out of her lungs. Surely Kyle wasn't telling the truth? David hadn't looked the type... She paused, confused and disturbed. Why was Kyle telling her this, anyway? She and David Hartley were nothing more than mere acquaintances!

But she had stupidly implied that out of that acquaintanceship a deep intimacy could easily grow, she admitted, angry with herself for her folly, and Kyle had always had an overdeveloped sense of responsibility where she was concerned.

She could still vividly remember the way he had waited up for her long after her parents had gone to bed, after her first adult 'teenage party'.

She was just about to make some comment when suddenly and clearly she heard a feminine voice in her ear.

'Kyle, darling,' it purred impatiently. 'How much longer are you going to be?'

'Heather...'

'Oh, don't let me keep you,' she said acidly. 'And please try to remember, Kyle, I'm not thirteen any more, and I don't need you to act the role of big brother and guardian of my morals.'

With that, she slammed the phone down, her good intentions forgotten. How dared he sit in judgement on David, when he was just as bad? What was she like, the woman who called him 'darling' so confidently?

It was none of her business, she chided herself. Besides, she was probably as anonymously beauti-

ful and plastic as all the other women who had
passed through his life.

As she went up to bed, she refused to allow
herself to think about him any more. She couldn't
help wishing, though, that he hadn't telephoned.
Hearing his voice had disturbed her, made her all
the more intimately aware of the fact that she was
now living in his home. It was a disturbing
awareness, and one she would rather not have had.
Much rather not have had!

CHAPTER SIX

HEATHER was up early, too keyed up about her father's operation to concentrate on anything, and yet knowing that there was no point in ringing the hospital so early. He wouldn't even be in the operating theatre yet.

She had sent him flowers and a telemessage, and although she ached to be with her mother she understood that this was a time when her parents wanted to be on their own.

They had always been very close, a wonderful example of how good and long lasting a relationship between two people could be.

At ten o'clock, when she was making her fourth cup of coffee of the morning, she heard a car outside and immediately rushed to the back door, just in time to see a small Ford car drive up.

The smartly dressed woman who slid from behind the wheel was around her own mother's age; but, whereas her mother's normal expression was one of cheerful enthusiasm, this woman's face was set in rather harsh and disapproving lines.

She smiled thinly when she saw Heather, and introduced herself. 'Vera Hartley. I believe you've already met my son.'

Heather had met enough possessive mothers in her time to recognise the breed, and even though she knew she was being unfair she couldn't help mentally contrasting David with Kyle. Kyle would never allow a mother, no matter how much adored, to run his life for him, where it seemed that David . . . but no, she was jumping to conclusions, based on information already put into her mind by Kyle. Perhaps it was unfair of her, but her original impression of David as a kind-hearted, attractive young man had been shadowed by Kyle's disclosure about his illegitimate child.

She knew that Kyle would never have misled her on such a subject, and it was disquieting to realise that such an apparently open and friendly person had a very much darker side to their nature. Of course, she would hardly have expected David to disclose such personal information on so short an acquaintance, but she had, nevertheless, a feeling of being let down in her judgement of his character.

There could be a dozen or more perfectly reasonable explanations of what Kyle had told her, but she was old-fashioned enough to find it disquieting to learn that David had been so easily able to dismiss his responsibilities.

Now she suspected she knew why. Vera Hartley looked the sort of woman who would want to choose her only son's wife herself, and weak men like David were notorious throughout history for involving themselves in liaisons that never gained that maternal approval.

'David explained to me that your van had broken down, and I thought I'd better drive round and check that you had everything you need.'

More like drive round and check up on *me*, Heather thought wryly.

'Yes, I'm fine, thanks. Please, do come in.' She had learned from her father how to deal with the most difficult kind of clients, and she used that knowledge to good effect now, putting aside her own feelings and assuming a mantle of cool good humour.

'Your father's in hospital, I understand,' Vera commented once they were both sitting down with mugs of coffee.

'Yes. He's undergoing surgery this morning. Naturally, we're all very concerned about him.'

'Mmm... And you and Kyle were virtually brought up together?' Vera's questions were beginning to ruffle Heather's assumed calm.

'My parents fostered Kyle, and he lived with us for a considerable number of years.'

'Mmm... so there isn't any actual *blood* tie between you, then? I must say I was surprised when I learned that you were coming to stay with him, but then I suppose your parents must know what they're doing. He certainly isn't the kind of man I'd want any daughter of mine to move in with.'

Before she knew how it had happened, Heather found that she was standing up, her whole body trembling with anger and resentment as she faced the other woman.

'I'm not exactly sure what you're trying to imply, Mrs Hartley,' she heard herself saying in an angrily tight voice, 'but quite frankly I think it's time you left, before I say something I might regret.'

It was on the tip of her tongue to tell the woman that, whatever Kyle's faults, he at least had never left a woman alone to bear his child, but just in time she caught the hasty impulse back.

She knew from the way Vera Hartley glared at her as she left that she had made a lifelong enemy,

but she didn't care. She was still trembling in the
aftermath of her shock at her own daring, and it
was only when the other woman had actually driven
away that Heather realised exactly what she had
done.

It was ironic, really, that she of all people should
have leapt too quickly to Kyle's defence. The
woman hadn't accused him of anything worse than
Heather herself had thought about him at one time
or another, and yet the resentment and fury she
had felt at hearing someone else run him down and
been so intense and real that they might almost have
been as close as any true brother and sister.

Although she didn't want to stray too far from
the house in case the phone rang, Heather spent a
brief half-hour exploring what she could of the
lovely formal Elizabethan gardens, the box hedges
now covered thickly in crisp white snow.

In the summer these gardens must be lovely. She
caught herself up just as she found herself wishing
she might be here to see it.

She had fallen in love with the house and its
setting, she admitted as she went back inside. There
was something so warm and homely about it, an
air of having been well loved and lived in, that
lingered almost as noticeably as the mingled scents
of potpourri and beeswax that permeated the air.

It was gone three in the afternoon before she received the long-awaited call, and Heather knew the
moment she heard her mother's voice that the operation had been a success. Her mother cried and
so did Heather; tears of thankfulness and gratitude.

'The specialist says that, with luck, your father
should be able to fly out to Portugal within a week.

He's still very woozy at the moment, and I'm going back to the guest house now, so I'll see you later, after you've picked up Kyle.'

They chatted for a few more moments, Heather telling her mother how lovely Kyle's home was, and putting her mother's rather obvious distraction down to the relief of knowing that her father's operation was at last over. Even so, she would have expected her mother to express rather more interest in Kyle's home; as it was, she seemed almost uninterested, almost as though Heather wasn't telling her anything she didn't already know.

It was half-past three when she put down the receiver, and almost immediately the phone rang again.

It caught her off guard to hear Kyle's voice. Knowing that he was returning home so soon, she hadn't expected to hear from him.

'Your father?' he questioned her tautly, without preamble. 'Is the operation . . . ?'

'Over and successful,' Heather responded, her own voice shaky as she recognised again how deep Kyle's love for her parents was.

'Thank God . . .'

He was only echoing her own thoughts, and yet for some reason the deep resonance of his voice made her eyes sting with tears.

'You'll be at the airport to meet me?'

'Yes, and then we can go straight to the hospital.'

Heather didn't want to drive Kyle's car for the first time in the dark, so after she had replaced the receiver she used the last half-hour of light in which to practise controlling the vehicle. It was an easy car to drive, light and responsive, and by the time she had driven up and down the drive several times, and neatly managed to reverse, she felt confident enough to turn off the engine and go back inside.

Oddly enough, her favourite downstairs room was the one Kyle had shown her, the one he used as his own study-cum-library, and it was in here that she lit the fire and settled down to flip through the daily paper, which so far she had left unread.

In addition to this room, the house had four other downstairs rooms, including a very lovely, south-facing drawing-room, decorated in soft peaches and blues, and a large formal dining-room.

The other two, best described as a sitting-room and a snuggery, were equally delightful, but it was in here, where she only had to close her eyes to imagine Kyle sitting opposite her, that Heather felt most at home.

Without being aware of it, her eyelids dropped, and the paper slid from her lap. It was the chiming of the grandfather clock outside in the hall that woke her, her shocked discovery that it was six o'clock making her rush upstairs to wash and change, before hurrying down again to have something to eat.

The very last thing she wanted was to be late for Kyle's flight. Hastily gulping down her hot coffee, she rang the airport to check that there were no delays. The paper was forecasting more snow, and it might be that Kyle's flight would have to be diverted.

Luckily, it seemed that so far Heathrow was clear of any fresh falls of snow.

The Jaguar had such an efficient heating system that Heather suspected she would be more than warm enough simply wearing the soft cream silk shirt and the straight navy wool skirt she had changed into, but just in case the flight was delayed and she had a long wait at Heathrow she added a toning navy jumper, embroidered with panthers' heads in a subtle silk-weave thread. The outfit had been an expensive one, but well worth every penny. She knew the navy contrasted well with the richness of the satin shirt, and that both threw into relief the lustre of her deep russet hair.

She had taken more care than usual over her make-up, and the image reflected by her mirror was rather more sophisticated than she was used to seeing. Her high heels made her taller than ever, but not tall enough to match Kyle, she admitted wryly.

She suspected that once she was working for him he would not look too kindly on her normal working 'uniform' of a tatty old track suit, and told herself that it was with this in mind that she was taking care with her appearance this evening, and nothing more.

It was snowing again as she left the house, large, fluffy flakes that floated majestically down to earth. Luckily, by the time she reached the motorway, it had stopped.

The temptation to drive faster than normal was something she subdued as she concentrated on controlling the powerful car, but even so she found that she reached London far sooner than she had expected.

At Heathrow, it took her some time to park the car, and she told herself that the nervous butterflies dancing in her stomach were the result of this complicated manoeuvre and had nothing to do with the fact that she was here to meet Kyle.

After checking the Arrivals board, she bought herself a cup of coffee and sat down to wait.

The moment she saw him, her heart turned over in her chest. It was an illuminating and shocking sensation, and one that held her rigid at the side of the barrier, her mouth dry with shocked fear, her body taut with the information that her mind refused to accept.

He came closer and she closed her eyes, willing the sensation of aching intensity to disappear. She could *not* feel like this about him, she would not *allow* herself to feel like this! She opened her eyes and, almost as though by magic, the feeling was gone. He was just Kyle, Kyle whom she had known for almost half her lifetime.

'Heather, what is it? Your father...?'

The harshness of his voice, the fierce way he gripped her shoulders, brought her back down to earth.

'He's fine,' she assured him, pushing away from him. 'How...how was your flight?'

'Fine.' He brushed her polite query aside impatiently. 'Then what the hell is wrong? You looked so white, I thought you were about to pass out.'

'Nothing's wrong.' Temper edged up under her voice. 'I've always been pale-skinned.'

She dreaded him pressing her any further. How on earth could she explain to him, or to anyone, in fact, that just for a moment as she'd looked at him, she had seen not the man she disliked and resented but instead a man whom she could very easily have loved? A man who aroused within her sensations she had never experienced for anyone else, sensations that were alien to her, and yet at the same time strangely familiar, as though in some past life she had known such a strength of feeling, and as though, too, Kyle himself was part of that shadowy, dim past.

Sheer imagination, she told herself, scoffing at the fantasy of her thoughts, as she directed Kyle to where she had parked his car.

It was only when his luggage was stowed in the boot and they were both inside it that she realised he expected *her* to drive. In the soft interior light of the car his face looked shadowed and drawn. Probably the result of too many late nights with the husky-voiced woman she had heard over the phone.

He leaned back in his seat as she started the car, his head turned away from her, as though he wished to ignore her presence, and so, stubbornly, Heather refused to break the silence.

It started to snow again as they reached the motorway, and she automatically dropped her speed. She felt Kyle turn to look at her and shift restlessly in his seat, and half expected him to demand that she stop the car so that he could take over.

Instead, to her shock he said quietly, 'You're a good driver.'

'For a woman, you mean?' she taunted, trying to subdue the spurt of pleasure his words gave her.

'No, that was *not* what I meant,' he responded tersely. 'Why is it that whenever I pay you a compliment, Heather, you throw it back in my face? Do you really detest me so much that you can't even accept a few words of praise from me?'

Was that how she seemed to him? She heard the tiredness in his voice and suppressed a faint sigh. As a child, she had grown up wary of his quick, clever tongue, and so she had taught herself to be mistrustful of everything he said. Now it seemed that she had been wrong.

'Seen much of Hartley, have you?'

She frowned and glanced at him, looking for signs of contempt, but his eyes were closed, his mouth a hard taut line.

'No,' she replied evenly, 'although his mother did call round this morning.'

'Ah ... warn you off, did she? She's very protective where her precious son is concerned.'

The bitterness in his voice was understandable, Heather acknowledged, especially in view of his own early childhood.

'I think it was more a recce than a warning-off exercise,' she told him good-humouredly. 'I must admit I don't envy the poor girl who will eventually become her daughter-in-law.'

'Does that mean you don't have any ambitions in that direction yourself?'

'After one meeting? Come on, Kyle!'

'And yet you seemed ready enough to leap to his defence,' he retorted smoothly.

'He was very kind to me,' she told him shortly. 'Kyle, is it true what you said about him having an illegitimate child?'

There was a hard silence and then he said coldly, 'What are you trying to ask me Heather? If I lied?'

'No. No, of course not. I know that you wouldn't. It's just that, sometimes, gossip can exaggerate.'

'This wasn't gossip. I know the girl concerned. She's the daughter of some friends of mine. Only eighteen and barely out of school. Hartley deliberately encouraged her infatuation with him. The poor little fool thought he was going to marry her. Of course, he denies the whole thing, and she, poor kid, is left with a ruined reputation and a child she can't bear to give up for adoption, when she's barely more than a child herself.'

It was a pitiful story, although not particularly uncommon, and Heather's tender heart ached for the other girl.

'As she's so young, perhaps it would be better for her if she moved away...had a fresh start.'

'That's what her parents would like her to do. They've offered to adopt and bring up her child, but the silly little idiot believes that he's going to go back to her. She's infatuated with him, as only an eighteen-year-old can be infatuated.' He frowned and glanced thoughtfully at her. 'You must have gone through that stage yourself?'

Had she? She must have done, but she couldn't remember it. Her hatred of Kyle had taken up so much emotional space in her life that there hadn't been any room left for anything else...or *anyone* else.

She shifted uncomfortably in her seat, frowning to herself. Had it really been like that? Had she really been so obsessed with Kyle that he had occupied all of her mental and emotional energy? Had resenting him really taken over so much of her life?

'I suppose I must,' she agreed carelessly.

'But in your case, without any lasting damage?'

She felt that he was pushing her to admit something, but had no idea what. She shrugged her shoulders, her eyes narrowing slightly as she concentrated on the snowy road.

'Obviously not.'

'Tell me, Heather, how many men *have* there been in your life since that first one?'

She was glad she was concentrating so hard on the road, otherwise she must surely have betrayed her shock. She willed herself not to look at him, nor to demand to know what business her personal life was of his.

'You can't honestly expect me to answer that,' she countered instead.

'Why not? If you were to ask me the same question, I'd answer it.'

'You mean you can remember them *all*?' she demanded drily.

She heard him laugh. 'You've been paying too much attention to the gossip columns. I could count on the fingers on one hand the number of serious emotional attachments I've had, and still have fingers over to spare.'

He was waiting for her to make some sort of response, but she had no idea what to say. The very thought of admitting to Kyle that, not only had there been no serious attachments, but also there had not been any *physical* attachments, made her skin shiver with goose-bumps.

'I... Oh, isn't that the sign coming up for our turn-off?' she questioned him thankfully, glad of a legitimate means of changing the conversation. 'I don't want to miss it, otherwise we'll be late for visiting time.'

'Your father's allowed open visiting hours, surely?' Kyle challenged, but to her relief he made no further attempt to direct their conversation into more personal channels.

They arrived at the hospital just as the nursing staff changed over. A small, smiling nurse directed them to her father's room. Although he was still wired up to a drip and monitoring machine, already his skin had a much healthier hue. Her mother stood up and rushed over to hug them both, tears thickening her voice as she welcomed them.

Heather stepped back for a moment as Kyle embraced her mother, unsure if she really wanted to probe the sensation of jealousy darting through her. Not jealousy of her mother's obvious love for Kyle, but jealousy of the look of concern and love in *Kyle's eyes* for her mother. Just for a moment she wished she was the one in his arms, that *she* was the one being comforted with the security of his caring.

Stop being so self-pitying, she chided herself briskly, turning away to give her father a final, lingering look before heading for the door.

'Don't worry. He'll be fine.'

Kyle's quiet words of reassurance startled her, and she looked round, half expecting to see that her mother had followed them out into the corridor and that they were for her, they held so much understanding and compassion.

But the corridor was empty apart from the two of them, and colour crawled betrayingly over her throat as she remembered how acutely perceptive Kyle had always been. Had he *seen* the look of lonely envy in her eyes as she'd watched him comfort her mother? She turned her head away, unaware of the sudden weary compression of his mouth as he watched her silent rejection of his words of comfort.

She had always been stubborn, yes, and proud too, and for a long time he had told himself that it was guilt and his love for her parents that had kept him away. But seeing her now, as a woman...

He cut the thought off, not wanting to pursue it.

'Come on, it's time we were on our way.'

Mutely, Heather followed him.

CHAPTER SEVEN

HEATHER and Kyle had been inside the hospital just over an hour, but during that time an alarming amount of snow had fallen. Already the car park was completely white, a sharp, mean wind blowing the flakes into ominous drifts.

One side of the Jaguar was almost completely white, and Kyle had to brush the snow away before they could get in.

It was still snowing, and the temperature had dropped. The air was crisp and cold, their breath sending small clouds of vapour into the darkness. Every time they moved, the snow that had already fallen crunched noisily underfoot.

'Would you prefer to drive?' Heather asked Kyle, but he shook his head.

'No, I'll leave it to you. Jet lag,' he added in explanation. He *did* look tired, she acknowledged, and oddly pale as well.

The main roads had been gritted, and they were lucky enough to be travelling during a lull in the traffic. Neither of them spoke; Heather was too busy concentrating on her driving to make polite small talk.

It seemed odd to be going home with Kyle, and yet it seemed right as well. Often during her teenage years he had picked her up from parties or dates. Then he had been the one driving, while she huddled resentfully in her head, keeping as much distance between them as possible. Out of the corner of her eye, she saw him shiver and automatically she reached out to boost the car heater.

'Are you all right?' The anxious words came out automatically.

'I'm fine.' He sounded so terse that she frowned again, sensing that he was lying.

'Kyle . . .'

'Don't fuss.' he told her sharply. 'It's just a bug I picked up in New York. Some sort of forty-eight-hour virus. I'll be all right in a few moments.'

He looked dreadful, she admitted worriedly, snatching another glance at him, but there was nothing she could do for him, other than get him home as quickly and as safely as possible.

Once off the main roads she had to slow down her speed and concentrate all her energies on manoeuvring the large car. Kyle had either gone to sleep or passed out, and she could only hope that it was the former.

When she eventually saw the turn-off for the village she felt quite limp with relief.

She was just turning into the now familiar drive when Kyle stirred and opened his eyes. He seemed to be having a problem recognising where he was, Heather realised, but then like a swimmer emerging from the sea he shook his head and sat up.

'You managed to get us back in one piece, then.'

This was more like the Kyle she knew, that sharp edge of mockery taunting her inability to be his equal.

'I did offer to let you drive,' she reminded him, equally acidly.

She had been going to ask him if he needed any help, but in view of the sharpness of his comment she judged that he must be feeling fully recovered, and so she went on ahead to unlock the door, leaving him to follow.

The snow was inches deep on the drive, the wind colder than ever now, cutting sharply through her clothes and bringing icy goose-bumps to her skin.

The warmth of the centrally heated house welcomed her inwards as she opened the outer door. Meg left her basket and came up to greet her. Heather looked back over her shoulder and saw that Kyle was still standing beside the car. She wavered on the threshold, uncertain as to whether to turn back to him or go in.

The abrupt dismissive wave he gave her made up her mind, and so she turned back to the house and left him to it. When he walked into the kitchen ten minutes later she was shocked by the exhaustion greying his face.

He sank heavily into one of the kitchen chairs, shivering convulsively, and this time she didn't bother to ask, but simply picked up the kettle and filled it with water.

She had no idea what sort of virus he had picked up, but a hot drink could only do him good.

He made no demur when she handed it to him, cradling his hands round the mug and drinking deeply.

Where he had been grey with exhaustion, now his face was flushed, drops of perspiration already beading his skin.

'It looks like 'flu,' Heather commented worriedly.

'Something similar,' he agreed briefly, and she sensed that he was trying to conserve what little energy he had left.

'You should have stayed in New York until you were over it.'

'I couldn't.' His eyes closed. 'I promised your father I'd be here in case you or your mother needed me.'

What could she say? How could she find the words to express the mingled feelings of guilt, pain and anger that filled her? How *could* she tell him that she didn't want his care of her to be commanded by her father, but to come from himself?

'I think you ought to go to bed,' she said flatly instead. 'I'll make you a hot water bottle and another drink, and bring them up.'

A little to her surprise, he got to his feet. His body swayed, and she reached out towards him instinctively, suppressing her skin's instinctive recoil from its electric contact with his. His forearm felt hard with bone and sinew, the skin dry and hot, the crispness of his dark hair alien to her sensitive fingertips.

As though he, too, disliked the contact, he pulled away grimacing, straightening up to walk past her and through the door.

She gave him ten minutes to get himself into bed, and then boiled water for the hot-water bottle she'd found in a drawer next to the sink. She made him another cup of tea, and then on impulse opened the fridge. As luck would have it, there were some lemons there. Good, when she came down she'd make him some proper lemonade, the kind her mother used to make and which he had always loved.

He was using the house's main bedroom, which had obviously been furnished and designed for a couple. The curtains hadn't been closed and, as she pulled them across the window, she noticed that the sky was clearing. Outside she heard the terrified screech of some small creature, followed by the triumphant hoot of an owl, and she shivered as she shut out the bright light of the silvered moon.

'You always were too sensitive for your own good,' Kyle said drowsily from the bed. 'Hunter...hunted...there's something of both in all of us, Heather, and you can't shut it out for ever.'

'I've brought you some more tea. Is there anything else you want? Aspirin...ought I to ring your doctor?'

Immediately he shook his head.

'It looks worse than it is, and adding a massive dose of jet lag to it doesn't help. I'll be all right in the morning.' He shivered again, and she moved instinctively towards the bed, to give him the hot-water bottle.

'You're going to make someone a wonderful mother,' he taunted drowsily as he took it from her. 'Why aren't you married already, Heather? Or have you been waiting for some wealthy young bucolic type like David Hartley to come along and sweep you off your feet? Be careful, he's no Prince Charming, and you'll have to get past his mother.'

Immediately, her sympathy for him vanished, and she glared furiously at him as she put his tea down.

'I'm not ready to get married yet, Kyle,' she told him acidly. 'I've still got far too many things I want to do. Besides, you're the one who should crave the cosiness of family life,' she gibed unkindly.

If he heard her he gave no sign of it, simply turning on his side and pulling the bedclothes up round his head.

Sighing faintly, Heather left. Why was it, whenever they seemed on the verge of actually making contact with one another, that something happened to drive them apart again? *Did* it just happen, she wondered soberly as she went downstairs to let Meg out for a final run, or was it manufactured? But if so, why, and by whom? Sometimes she knew that she was the one at fault, her defence system springing into action to protect her against the old remembered wounds Kyle had once inflicted, but sometimes he was the one at fault, and surely he had nothing to fear from her?

She opened the kitchen door, and Meg dashed out without waiting for her to pull her boots on.

It was freezing now, the cold turning the snow-shrouded trees into fantasy spectres straight out of a fairy-tale. While Meg investigated the magical white stuff that covered the ground, Heather watched a cautious squirrel. It froze the moment it saw them, tiny beady eyes holding Heather's, as though willing her not to attack.

Meg came bustling through the snow-covered undergrowth, crackling and panting, and the tiny creature disappeared. Meg's nose was covered in snow and she grinned happily up at Heather, her plumy tail waving.

'Come on . . . time to go in.'

She had loved the house when she had it to herself, but now, with Kyle sleeping upstairs, she felt somehow as though it was even more of a home. Perhaps because of what Kyle had said to her, perhaps not, she didn't know, but as she tidied up the kitchen and settled Meg and the cats for the night, she couldn't help peopling the room with small faces and excited little voices: children who would love this house, who would be privileged to grow up here in its freedom.

Sighing faintly, she banished the mental images, uncomfortably aware that she had furnished them with Kyle's dark hair and eyes.

She switched off the lights and went upstairs. Outside Kyle's room, she paused. Her hand touched the doorhandle and then fell away. If he needed her he would call, and yet it had been hard to suppress her instinctive urge to go in and check that he was all right.

Because that was the way she had been brought up, she told herself drily. That was all, there was nothing more personal in her desire to check up on him; it had no bearing at all on that odd frisson of sensation that had raced through her when she had accidently touched his skin.

She slept heavily and late, and was woken by the ring of her alarm. She sat up, switching it off, swinging her feet to the floor and looking sleepily for her robe.

She was just about to walk into her bathroom when she heard the telephone ringing downstairs.

Immediately, the thought of her father and the possibility of a relapse sent her flying downstairs, but when she eventually picked up the receiver it was only to discover that it was a wrong number.

The day was clear and crisp, with a blue winter sky and a pale yellow sun. Letting Meg out, Heather set off back upstairs to shower and dress.

She was just passing Kyle's door when he called out to her. She opened it and went in.

He was still standing beside his bed, and she automatically averted her glance from the hair-roughened nudity of his torso.

She had surely seen him like this before at some time or another, clad only in a brief pair of briefs, because somehow part of her mind registered the sight of him as a familiar one. But in those days he could scarcely have been so... so male, she thought weakly, wishing that she had the *savoir-faire* to coolly shrug off her awareness of him.

'I heard the phone, was it the hospital?'

'No... just a wrong number. How are you feeling this morning?'

'Weak as a cat.' He grimaced and, as though to prove it, as he started to move, he seemed to lose his balance.

Heather rushed towards him instinctively, catching him just as he fell heavily towards the bed. She was pinned beneath the full weight of his upper body, his chest crushing her, her face pressed into the hot arch of his throat.

She could feel a pulse beating erratically against her mouth. Her senses swam, reality as unwelcome as envisaging last night's fairy-tale snow-covered branches denuded of their beautifying white blanket and left bare and stark.

Afterwards, she wasn't sure which of them moved first; whether it was she who wrapped her arm tightly around Kyle's neck, or he who groaned despairingly into her hair and cupped his hands against the back of her head, his lips moving to her ear as he demanded rawly, 'Open your mouth, kiss me, Heather.' His whole body surged against her as she complied mindlessly, filled with the pleasure of tasting his skin, of being free to explore the solid arch of his throat with all its tastes and textures, and with a hunger inside her so deep that there was no way she could block out the knowledge that she must have, with some part of her, wanted this intimacy for an aeon of time.

His hand cupped her breast, ruthlessly pushing aside both her robe and her nightgown, seeking the warmth of her flesh with a compulsion that echoed her own. Part of her knew and recognised it and responded to it as well, the sensation of his hands on her body making her arch up in eagerness as surge after surge of primitive delight washed through her.

'You like me touching you like this...and like this?'

His voice, the hoarse passion of the words he muttered in her ear excited her senses, orchestrating her responses. Somehow she was free of her clothes. Free to run her hands over the hard velvet of his skin, free to revel in the exquisite sensation of flesh against flesh. Her body flowered, bloomed in his touch. His mouth caressed her. His weight pressed her to the bed, imprisoning her, and yet she knew she had no desire to escape. The heat of him, the hard pulsing urgency of his manhood, these were things she had never known before, and yet her body welcomed them as though they were long familiar to her. Even the scent of his arousal excited her, as though in some curious way it had an aphrodisiac effect long known to her and mourned in his absence.

Later she would be shocked, shattered, in fact, by her reaction to him, appalled that she had not fought to prevent it, and confused by how easily she had slipped out of her familiar mould and into one she herself could not recognise.

His tongue-tip stroked her skin, his whole body trembling with the need she could feel pulsing through him. Soon she would feel the heat of his mouth against her breast, soon he would...

The sharp sound of a vehicle outside cut through her rising desire for him. Both of them tensed.

'Hartley,' Kyle said thickly, pulling away from her. 'I'd recognise that Land Rover of his anywhere.'

Cold air rushed over her skin as Kyle moved, and immediately she was as conscious of her nudity as Eve after she had taken that first bite at the apple. An apt simile, for like Eve she had wantonly tasted forbidden fruit!

She rushed to pick up her discarded things, while Kyle said laconically, 'No need to rush, he's only at the bottom of the drive.'

'Kyle...'

He heard the anguish in her voice and laughed.

'Oh, it's all right, I'm not going to betray you to him, if that's what worrying you. He's not exactly pure as the driven snow himself, you know.'

She tried again. 'Kyle!'

'Oh, for God's sake, stop acting like a Victorian virgin!' he derided her. 'It's not the end of the world. We both knew it would happen some time.' He looked wryly at her. 'It's always been there between us, after all. I don't think there's been a single woman I've taken to bed who I haven't at one time or another mentally compared to you...'

Heather stared at him, appalled both by his cynicism and what he was revealing.

'No... no... that's not true!'

'Oh, come on, Heather.' Impatience deepened his voice. 'OK, I admit that when you were a teenager you probably couldn't recognise all that aggression between us for what it was, but you're not a kid any more. You must be as able to recognise desire as I can myself. All right, I had an advantage. I knew then that I wanted you. I tried to tell myself it was because you were forbidden fruit, but you've haunted me for years, making me ache in a way that no one else can.'

'But we don't even like one another.'

He shrugged. 'So what? You must know that it's possible to be driven mad by a need of someone you don't particularly like.'

She could sense a tension about him she hadn't noticed earlier, and his eyes were shielded from her, almost as though there was something there he didn't want her to read, but panic clawed at her and she was in no mood for rational analysis. She had to get out of his room, she had to get back to reality and sanity and to the safety of a world where Kyle was just a man whom she disliked, instead of the one man in the whole world who had the ability to make her feel that nothing else mattered other than being in his arms.

These were feelings she had always associated in her mind with the word 'lover', with the sort of relationship shared by her parents, but as Kyle had just cynically pointed out, *they* did not even like one another.

Appalled, almost horrified, Heather picked up her things and fled.

By the time she had pulled on a jumper and jeans she discovered why it had taken David so long to get up the drive. His Land Rover was towing a small snow-plough and he had cleared the drive for them.

If he hadn't arrived when he had, by now she and Kyle... She swallowed hard, trying to banish the tormenting image.

'Well, haven't you got a reward for my hard endeavours?' David Hartley demanded cheerfully as she opened the kitchen door to both him and Meg.

Forcing a smile, she invited him in. Behind her she heard Kyle enter the kitchen, and instantly she was so aware of him that the small hairs on her scalp stood up.

He came over to join them, menacing her somehow. Even David was aware of something, because he frowned and checked himself and gave them both a speculative look.

'Actually, I came to see if you fancied going out for a drink with me tonight?'

'Heather doesn't.'

'I'd love to go with you,' she said quickly, overruling whatever it was Kyle had been about to say. 'What time?'

'I'll pick you up about eight.'

She could sense Kyle's disapproval, and she was so acutely aware of him still that she also picked up on his sexual jealousy.

Kyle, jealous of David? She shivered, and tried to stem the flood of primitive pleasure rushing through her. This was madness! She was playing with fire. There could never be any real sort of relationship between her and Kyle, and to have one based on the sort of sexual intensity they had just generated was so appallingly dangerous that she automatically dismissed it. No, she didn't want to fall into that sort of trap. Instinctively she fought against what she knew would be dangerous to her, trying to dismiss the feelings Kyle had aroused in her, trying to convince herself that they had been born out of anxiety and proximity.

It was obvious from Kyle's silence, once David had gone, that he was furious with her, but stubbornly Heather refused to be the first to break it. It was no concern of Kyle's whom she dated, just because...just because they had almost been lovers. She shied away from the word physically, just as she shied away emotionally from what was happening to her.

It was Kyle who eventually broke the silence, saying heavily, 'Heather, we have to talk.'

'No!' Panic hit her, she didn't want to talk about what had happened. It was shaming enough that it simply had. 'No, no, I don't want to talk... What happened this morning...it's over...I just want to forget it...'

She saw his mouth tighten, and for a moment she held her breath, frightened by the contempt she saw in his eyes, but then he turned away and shrugged.

'If that's the way you want it. You never did like facing up to anything, did you, Heather? I suppose I should have expected something like this. I'm going out.'

'You're not well enough,' she protested.

'Well, let me put it to you this way,' he told her, rounding on her, his eyes dark, glittering with the intensity of his anger. 'If I stay here and I can't get through to you any other way, I might...I just might be tempted to take you right back to my bed and show you...' He broke off, making a harsh sound of disgust deep in his throat. 'Oh, for God's sake, what's the use? I've got work to do. If you hear from the hospital, I'll be in my study...I take it we *are* still going to see your parents this afternoon?'

That was the arrangement they had made, and Heather nodded her head, confused by both his attitude and his comments. What was it he had been going to say? That he could take her to bed and overcome her scruples? That he could make her want him with the same mind-destroying intensity she had experienced this morning? She already knew that. Why else was she so terrified of letting him get too close to her? Why else was she so determined to put up barriers against him? How long had her body secretly wanted him as its lover? How long had she needed him like that? How long would she need him? It was a frighteningly appalling prospect to want a man with such a physical intensity, and with a need that seemed to turn her off all other members of the male sex, when she knew there was no love, no respect, no softer, gentler emotions of any sort between them.

David was her armour against him, she recognised. David was her only means of keeping him at bay, because once he knew that there had been no other man, that he only had to touch her and she melted with longing for his possession . . . once he knew that . . . She shivered; she would never allow Kyle to become her lover. She would never open herself to the emotional pain that such a relationship would bring. Never!

CHAPTER EIGHT

As she stared around her father's hospital room, Heather was acutely conscious of a feeling of constraint and nervousness. She couldn't even look at Kyle, and yet at the same time she was desperately afraid that her parents, especially her mother, would guess that something was wrong and start to question her.

Amazingly, her mother appeared not to notice how jumpy and tense she was, and she put it down to the fact that she was still quite naturally concentrating all her attention on her father.

Kyle knew, though. The cool, mocking glances he gave her whenever she dared to look at him informed her of that. How adept he was at concealing and controlling his emotions! Looking at him now, witnessing that taunting curl of his mouth, who could ever imagine that not so very long ago that mouth...

Abruptly she turned her head away, her face flushing as she was swept by an unwelcome surge of physical desire.

'You look hot, Heather, are you all right?'

Of course, it would be *now* that her mother suddenly became maternal and concerned, and Heather could see in the sardonic smile Kyle gave her that he knew quite well what had caused that brilliant wave of heat to surge over her skin.

Today her father looked even better; he was participating far more in the conversation, and some of the machines had been taken away. He was now out of intensive care and talking enthusiastically to them about how much he was looking forward to going to Portugal.

Her parents knew the part of the country where Kyle's villa was situated very well. It was right down by the Spanish border, quiet and still, virtually untouched by tourism.

Listening to the three of them talking, Heather was conscious once more of being shut out, but for once she didn't mind. It gave her an opportunity to strengthen her defences. But against what? An attack on her virtue? She shuddered a little, remembering how easily Kyle had been able to arouse her. Too easily.

'Heather, come back! You were miles away.'

With a small start, she looked at her mother.

'Probably thinking about her date tonight,' Kyle drawled.

'A date? Who with?' her mother asked curiously. 'A...'

'Our local Lothario,' Kyle interrupted before she could explain. 'I made the mistake of warning Heather against him. I should have remembered that any advice from me was likely to have the opposite effect to that intended.'

'Oh, Heather, do you think you're being wise?' her mother reproached her anxiously. 'If Kyle is right about this young man...'

'I'm meeting him for a drink, Mum, that's all.' Over her mother's head, Heather glowered at her persecutor. Kyle was enjoying this, damn him! Just for a moment she longed to rip the mask of illusion from her mother's eyes and tell her exactly how Kyle himself had treated her, but the temptation faded just as quickly as it had come, leaving her feeling weak and shaky. Why was it that Kyle had this ability to push her far, far beyond the limits of sanity and into a dangerous mood of reckless intensity?

'David seemed a perfectly respectable young man to me,' she challenged, glaring at Kyle. 'His mother is rather overpowering, mind you.'

'His mother? You've met her?'

'Yes, she came round the other morning. They're farmers, and Kyle's closest neighbours.'

'And Mama Hartley is as protective of her one and only as a ewe with one lamb,' Kyle interrupted derisively. 'His wife, when he's allowed to marry, will be hand-picked by Mama, but in the mean time she turns a blind eye while he amuses himself with anyone stupid or innocent enough not to see through him.'

A sharp cough from her father brought Heather back to reality. She bit her lip, resenting Kyle for pushing her into such an argumentative frame of mind. Her father should be her main concern at the moment, and not her relationship with Kyle.

They left half an hour later. The next time she saw her parents would be when she and Kyle collected them to drive them to the airport. She and Kyle had seen her father's specialist before leaving the hospital, and he had assured them that her father was perfectly able to undergo the flight.

'A few weeks relaxing in a pleasant climate will do far more to help him recuperate than being cooped up in a hospital room. You've taken the sensible precaution of hiring a nurse to travel with him, and she'll see him safely installed in your villa. We've made arrangements with the local hospital, and a local doctor will call and check on him every day.

Until that moment, Heather hadn't known that Kyle had hired a nurse to accompany her parents on the flight.

She looked up at him now, as he drove the Jaguar back towards his home.

Her words of thanks sounded stilted even to her own ears, her throat felt sore and rough, taut with resentment because yet again he had done something selfless and thoughtful, and in doing so had destroyed the image of him she was trying so hard to build up. She wanted to view him in the worst possible light. She needed to because that was the only way...

Her thoughts skidded to a standstill as she refused to contemplate where they were leading.

'Heather, cancel your date with Hartley tonight.'

The abrupt request, coming so close on the heels of a realisation she wasn't yet ready to accept, made her tense and reject his suggestion without even considering it.

'I don't interfere in your personal life, Kyle,' she snapped acidly. 'I'm not seventeen any more, you know. I'm perfectly capable of dealing with any unwanted advances.'

'Are you?'

She opened her mouth, a vigorous confirmation already on her lips and then closed it again. If she answered him as she wished to, mightn't he then assume that she had actually *wanted* him to make love to her?

The frustration of her dilemma showed in her eyes, and Kyle, who was watching her, suppressed the bitter words clamouring for utterance. He had forgotten how stubborn she could be, how stubborn and how proud. It was useless to wish that time could roll back and that one could re-live the past in order to wipe out its mistakes.

Heather hated and resented him. He should be able to accept that by now. Instead he ... Impatient with both himself and the irony of his feelings, he compressed his mouth, and Heather, catching sight of that hardening of his facial bones, told herself fiercely that she was glad that she hadn't betrayed herself to him; glad that they were still enemies.

It was only later, when she was getting ready for her date with David, that she questioned what it was she feared she might betray, but she brushed to one side the encroaching little voice that asked the question, dismissing it as too intrusive and demanding.

David arrived just as she went downstairs. She had dressed casually for their date, in a softly gathered russet-coloured wool skirt with a toning sweater worn over a cream silk blouse.

'Very country,' Kyle drawled when he saw her. 'Who is it you're hoping to impress, David or his mother?'

His derision stung, and she hurried past him, not trusting herself to make any response. No doubt he preferred women dressed in designer silks and lace, in clothes that emphasised the perfection of bodies honed by hours of pampering. She wasn't that sort of woman, and she never would be.

The pleased glance of approval that David gave her soothed her lacerated senses. His solicitous care as he helped her into his Land Rover made her think that Kyle must have been exaggerating in describing his attitude towards the female sex.

The pub was several miles away, isolated and exposed to the worst of the winter weather, but nevertheless it seemed well patronized, to judge from the full car park.

Several people greeted David as they walked in, most of the greetings coming from a group by the bar.

As David introduced her, Heather was conscious of several overt smirks from one or two of the other men present. Instinctively, she disliked this male gathering and its almost schoolboy humour, although she tried to temper her rejection of it by reminding herself that her upbringing and life had been such that she wasn't used to this particular aspect of the male psyche. Her father and mother rarely went out socially without one another, and not having had any siblings, and being rather a quiet and withdrawn sort of child, she had never been drawn into the sort of environment where she might have witnessed this type of male 'ganging up'.

Kyle, like her, had always been something of a loner. He had made friends, it was true, but looking back she could see that he had always held them at something of a distance.

Now, while David was welcomed into the heart of the almost exclusively male group, Heather found that she was left on its fringes, forced to make awkward and unwanted conversation with the two other girls present.

One of them was a small blonde mouse of a child, who seemed to have no opinions of her own and who apparently needed to corroborate everything she had to say by appealing to her boyfriend for confirmation.

The other, a tall, striking brunette, appeared to be as bored by the exclusively male conversation as she was herself, and Heather quickly discovered that she was not here with a boyfriend, but her brother.

'I was staying in tonight and at something of a loose end. When Guy suggested I join him I agreed, forgetting what bores ex-public schoolboys can be at times.' She made a face. 'I live and work in London and I'm just home for a few days' holiday. This isn't my scene, really. I suspect it isn't yours, either?'

'Not really,' Heather agreed, turning to answer an almost inevitable, 'Have you known David long?' from the mousey blonde at her other side.

'No, I haven't. He rescued me the other night when my car broke down.'

'You don't live locally, then?' she persisted.

'Not normally, at the moment I'm staying with a...a friend. Kyle Bennett.'

The blonde's shocked expression might have been amusing in other circumstances, and Heather could almost have sworn she moved two paces away from her, as though distancing herself from someone carrying some sort of dread disease.

Written large in her expressive and ingenuous blue eyes were the words 'fast and dangerous'.

How amusing that *she* of all people, should be so judged! How amusing, and how untrue.

The brunette was obviously made of sterner stuff. Her eyebrows lifted a little, but her only comment was a rather envious one.

'Kyle Bennett. I've heard of him of course, but never actually met him. Are you...old friends?'

'You could say so.' Some touch of mischief stopped Heather from explaining too much. 'I've known him since I was...oh, in my early teens.'

'Really...'

Susie, the little blonde, moved a little closer. 'Your parents were friends with his or something, then, were they?'

Quite what made her do it Heather didn't know, perhaps it was the self-confident, irritating air of the men standing behind them, perhaps it was something she had read in Susie's curious eyes, she didn't know. She only knew that she was as appalled as Susie looked when, instead of explaining, she said carelessly instead, 'Oh, no, I've never met Kyle's family. We...lived together for quite some time, but he left and we'd rather lost touch until quite recently.'

Strictly speaking, it was the truth, but Heather was well aware of the connotation that would be put on her revelations. She was right as well.

Behind her the hum of male voices stilled, and as she turned her head she caught David looking at her with an odd, calculating expression in his eyes.

Claire, the brunette, broke the silence by saying casually, 'I'd like to meet him. I believe he's a most interesting man.'

'Very interesting,' Heather agreed, mentally thanking her for the lifeline. 'In fact, one of the reasons I'm here now is that I'm shortly to start work for him.'

She could see that none of them believed her. Behind her, one of the men made a soft comment to his companions, and the appreciative male laughter it caused made the back of her neck burn scarlet with temper and mortification.

The evening couldn't end too quickly for her after that, and when, at half-past ten David suggested that they leave, she was all too happy to comply.

She caught one of the suggestive leers his friends gave him, but ignored it, following him out into the crisp, icy coldness of the winter night.

It had been warm inside the pub, and she shivered as she waited for him to unlock the Land Rover door.

They seemed to have been travelling for an awfully long time, she realised half an hour later. Surely it hadn't taken them this long to reach the pub?

Just as she was about to comment, she saw a crop of buildings ahead of them and expelled her breath in relief. Until then she hadn't known that she was actually feeling tense, but now she recognised that Kyle's warning had taken root and had grown rapidly as she'd listened to the men's conversation.

Her relief was short-lived, however, as she realised that the outline of the buildings was unfamiliar to her.

'David . . . ?'

'Don't worry... it's a farmhouse we own, no one actually lives here, so we won't be disturbed.'

For a moment his casual manner almost deceived her, and then, as she turned towards him, she read the cold-blooded intention in his eyes and shrank back from him.

'David, I think you've made a mistake,' she said as evenly as she could. 'Please take me home.'

'Oh, come on.' How quickly he had changed from the charming young man into this leering threatening stranger. 'It's too late to pretend now. And it isn't as though it's going to be the first time. Lived with Bennett, did you? Well, he should have taught you a trick or two well worth knowing.'

She reached blindly for the door, but he beat her to it, taking her wrist in a painful grip.

'David, stop this... I don't...'

'Want me?' he laughed sourly. 'You will, I promise you. Bennett can't be that good in bed.'

What she was hearing horrified her, and if she had had any doubts about David's intentions, these were swiftly banished when he cursed her obscenely under his breath and told her explicitly and graphically just what he expected of her.

It was like a nightmare, and she struggled to hold on to some measure of calm. David couldn't force her to go into the farmhouse with him. She was safer staying here in the Land Rover. She was long past believing that he was far too civilised to want a woman he had to force into making love with him. She had read in his eyes his determination, and suspected that it sprang as much as anything from a boast made to his cronies that he could do so.

It was a type of male attitude that had always sickened her, and now it frightened her as well. She had read about women being raped by men whom they knew, but she had never, ever expected it to happen her. But it would, if she didn't do something...

If only she could get David to leave her alone in the Land Rover... She could drive off then and leave him. But how?

There was only one way. Gritting her teeth, she forced a smile. She was going to play a role she had never, ever even envisaged playing, and the whole of the rest of her life would depend upon how successfully she played it.

'Kyle is good,' she agreed, trying to sound both coy and promising, closing her mind to the sickening sense of despair eating into her as revulsion for what she was doing hit her.

'That's more like it.' A self-satisfied smile curved the weak mouth. Oh, *why* hadn't she listened to Kyle. *Why* had she allowed her headstrong self-will to overrule his cautioning?

'Come on, let's go inside.'

She looked wildly into the dark stretch of ground that lay between them and the house, and then inspiration struck.

'You go first... it's dark... it... it scares me.'

She gave a realistic shudder.

'I'll turn on the headlights.'

'Then you'll have to come back and switch them off... I'm scared of strange places. It's so remote and... and wild up here. You scare me, too,' she added softly, sickened by the look of pleasure and gloating darkening his eyes, hating herself for what she was being forced to stoop to.

'All right...but first I want a taste of what you've been giving Bennett.'

He grabbed her before she could stop him, and Heather had to force herself not to push him away. If she fought him now she would lose everything she had been working towards. Even so, her throat tightened and locked against a rising wave of sickness as his mouth fastened over hers. His hands were inside her jacket, rough and unskilled as they touched her breasts.

She endured it for as long as she could, hating the soft sounds of his breathing and the oppressive heat of his body.

'I'm cold...' she protested when she couldn't stand it any longer. 'Let's go inside.'

'Come on, then...'

She shook her head in what she hoped was a coquettish and promising way.

'No, you go first. I'll wait until you've got the lights on... I'm scared.'

Later, she could only think that it was his monstrous vanity that had saved her; that and the fact that he simply couldn't imagine that she couldn't secretly want him, otherwise he would surely never have left her alone.

She waited until he had almost reached the house, straining her eyes to make out his black shadow in an equally deep pool of blackness, before starting the Land Rover engine.

Luckily it fired the first time, but she was not prepared for the speed with which he raced back towards her, or the force with which he wrenched open the driver's door, clawing at her as he tried to drag her out.

She screamed, and then, realising that it was a waste of energy, she concentrated instead on maintaining her hold on the steering wheel. Luckily, by some miracle he had left the Land Rover in gear and so, crunching the gear-box horribly, she was able to set the vehicle in motion. As she turned it into a circle, not caring what might be in her way in the form of fences or walls, David still hung on to her arm. The pain from the biting grasp of his fingers made her long to lift both hands from the wheel and push at him, but she forced herself not to give in to it. His other hand clawed at her blouse, tearing the soft fabric. He kicked hard at her right leg, trying to dislodge her from the controls, and then thankfully the engine started to pick up speed.

He hung on to her for far longer than she had imagined possible, and she had visions of dragging his inert body with her for the rest of her life, but suddenly he let go. She heard the dull thud as he fell to the ground, but dared not stop to check if he was all right.

By some miracle she found the main road, not caring where it took her as long as it was away from David, but eventually she discovered she was heading in the right direction for the village.

It took her another twenty minutes to reach Kyle's home.

The front of the house was in darkness. It was still only half-past eleven, but Kyle must have gone to bed. Thank God for that. The last thing she wanted was for him to see her in this state.

As she stopped the Land Rover and tried to climb out, she discovered that her legs were almost too stiff to obey her, partly from shock and partly from the pain in the one David had kicked. Something warm and sticky ran down inside her ruined blouse, and she dragged herself towards the front door with the slow, halting steps of a very, very old woman.

Just as she reached the door, she felt a wave of faintness wash over her. She fought desperately to control it, one hand clutching at the door, the other searching despairingly in her bag for her key.

When the door unexpectedly opened inwards the shock on top of so many other shocks was too much for her. She gave a harsh, terrified scream and then collapsed inwards in a dead faint.

Kyle caught her, his body jarred by the unexpected weight of her. He had been working in his study earlier in the evening and had fallen asleep, the remains of his jet lag catching up with him. The sound of the Land Rover had woken him, and he had come to the door to investigate.

Now, as he studied Heather's white face and bruised body, a feeling of rage, so intense and all consuming that it threatened to overcome everything else, enveloped him.

The last time he had felt this anger had been when Heather had tried to kill herself. Then it had been directed inwards at himself. Now...

He carried her towards the sitting-room, and then changed his mind and headed for the stairs.

She came round just before he placed her on his bed, her eyes wild and frantic until they focused on his face, and terror faded. As they closed, he bit back the questions rioting inside him. Time enough for questions later, all but one.

'Where is he?'

The harsh demand penetrated Heather's fogged mind. She didn't open her eyes, but turned her head in Kyle's direction instead.

'He took me to a farm...it's...it's empty...I left him there.'

'Yes, I know it.' He looked down at her, torn between two equally fierce needs, and in the end the more gentle of them won. He knew the farmhouse Heather meant quite well. It was remote and without a telephone. Unless Hartley decided to walk, he would be stuck there until daylight.

At that moment Heather opened her eyes again, her lashes fluttering weakly as though too heavy for her frailty to support.

Her fingers touched his sleeve and trembled against it, and as though she had read his mind she whispered huskily, 'Kyle, don't leave me.'

Heather heard herself say the words and was shocked by them; nearly as shocked as she had been by the expression of fierce rage in Kyle's eyes.

From the past, her memory dredged up a taunt once thrown at her by a jealous schoolfriend. 'He isn't really your brother, and you're in love with him, aren't you?'

How fiercely she had denied it, how hard she had worked to prove to the world and to herself how much she disliked him. So much wasted energy, she reflected tiredly, so much mental torment and self-inflicted pain, and all for what? All to bring her to this point in her life when she was confronted with a dead end, with the truth she had fought so long to deny.

She loved Kyle. No wonder she had responded so quickly and so intensely to him. No wonder her flesh had quickened to his touch. No wonder she had hidden the truth from herself for so long.

Weak tears rushed into her eyes. Like a small, betrayed creature she wanted to crawl under the protection of a large rock and hide there until the danger had gone. Only it would never go. If she had mistaken the true nature of her feelings for Kyle at seventeen, she couldn't mistake them now.

Tonight, trapped in the Land Rover with David, forced to confront her total revulsion towards him, she had had an illuminating mental image of Kyle, and she had seen him then not as her enemy, not as her unwanted adopted brother, but as a man. And not just any man; the man to whom everything within her that made her feminine instinctively turned, physically, mentally and emotionally.

She shivered beneath the knowledge, too weak to evade it as she had done so many times in the past. Where another teenager, given the same feelings, might have betrayed them, and thus worked through them, she had refused to admit them and had hidden them away so that they had grown and were now threatening to take over her whole life.

She groaned, and Kyle, hearing and mistaking the sound, swore. Listening to him, Heather flinched at the violence she could feel him containing. She moved and the light fell on her bruised leg.

Kyle touched it. His hand trembled slightly and she tensed. Was he, then, so furious with her that he was practically shaking with rage?

He had warned her and she had ignored him. She was lucky to have got off with little more than bruises and a bad fright.

'I'm sorry.'

The humble apology that once would have made her cringe with self-contempt was a plea for understanding as well as forgiveness.

'*You're* sorry! I shouldn't have let you go with him. I should have...' He broke off and said quietly, 'Listen to me, Heather, because I think I can only say this once. God knows, neither of us is able to be detached about this. If Hartley... if he raped you, it's a matter for the police. You must tell me...'

She shook her head vehemently.

'No...no, he didn't, although I've no doubt that was what he intended once he realised that I wasn't...' She broke off and shuddered, her body going hot and then cold with the reality of how easily she could have been saying exactly the opposite.

'I...I managed to fool him into getting out of the Land Rover... I started to drive off.' She shuddered again, more tensely this time, the mental image of how he had clung and torn at her flesh still too real.

'He tried to drag me out of the Land Rover...I...I thought he was going to...and then he let go. I heard him fall.' She struggled to sit up, burying her head against Kyle's shoulder, her voice shaking with remembered fear. 'Kyle, I don't know what happened to him. I don't think I ran over him or...'

'He'll be all right,' Kyle told her curtly. 'His kind always are.' His hand slipped round her throat, tilting her chin so that he could look at her face, and then, as his thumb brushed against the spot where she was bleeding, he frowned.

'It's nothing...just a scratch.'

'I ought to take you to hospital.'

'No...no, please.' She shrank from the suggestion like a night creature from the light. She couldn't bear to be questioned and pulled this way and that. 'I'll be all right once I've had a bath.'

She tried to get off the bed, but Kyle restrained her.

'Heather,' he said soberly. 'If Hartley did...if he did rape you, you have nothing to feel ashamed about, you know that, don't you? You...'

'Kyle, I've already told you I'm still the same boring twenty-three-year-old virgin I was before...' She broke off, her face going white as she recognised the shock in his eyes. Her skin burned, her body frozen into tension. What had she said? Oh, that stupid, idiotic tongue of hers. What on earth had possessed her to make that flip, acid response without thinking about what she was saying?

She waited for what seemed to be a lifetime, already anticipating Kyle's sarcastic remark, her tension increasing when he said nothing. Either he didn't believe her and didn't want to say so, or he did believe her and pitied her so much that he was passing up on the opportunity to mock her. Neither alternative pleased her.

'Kyle...'

'We'd better get those cuts and bruises seen to,' he interrupted brusquely. 'Can you make it to the bathroom, or would you like a hand?'

How frightening that should feel so bereft, so forlorn. What had she expected, that he would pick her up tenderly and carry her there?

'I can manage on my own.'

She hated the way he stepped back from her, almost as though he disliked the thought of being in physical contact with her. In another man she might have suspected his withdrawal sprang from a distaste of touching her because of David Hartley, but Kyle wasn't like that. Already he had exhibited his compassion and understanding. Too weary to analyse his reaction, Heather stumbled towards the bathroom door.

'Heather, let me . . .'

She rounded on him fiercely. 'I'm all right. I can manage.'

She slammed the door behind her, leaving him on the other side. Her head was swimming and her body felt so weak; an after-effect of the shock and fear she had experienced, she suspected.

She showered quickly, grimacing over the scratches and bruises marring her skin. She was unfortunate in that she bruised easily. Too easily, she thought, dismayed by the purpling patches of swollen skin. No wonder Kyle had doubted her assertion that David had barely touched her.

He was waiting for her when she opened the door, a grim expression on his face and a tray with a glass of water and two tablets on it in his hand.

'These are very mild sleeping tablets. My doctor prescribed them for me last year.'

'For you? But . . .'

'Too many flights across the Atlantic,' he told her brusquely. 'I got too wound up and couldn't wind down.'

There was no point in telling her the rest of it, in describing that sickening sensation of desolation that had undermined his physical strength and had left him feeling as though life was little more than a dreary round of duty and obligation. There had even been a time... He grimaced faintly. There was little point in dwelling on life's ironic and often unkind twists. He held out the glass to Heather. 'Here, drink this.'

One part of her wanted to object. The other knew she needed the healing benefit of a sound night's sleep.

She took the water, and one of the tablets, shaking her head in refusal of the second.

'They normally work within half an hour,' Kyle told her. 'Can you make it to your own room? Or . . .'

'I can make it.'

The compassion, and with it the bond she had sensed earlier, were gone now and he was once again the Kyle of her childhood, but now there was a subtle difference—not in him but in her. *Now* he was the man she loved as well.

Acknowledging that love had been a painful, slow progress, a story of denials and rejections that had brought her loneliness and misery. And now that she *had* faced up to the truth?

She could see no future in her feelings for Kyle, she admitted sleepily. He did not return her love and it was hardly likely that he ever could. Drowsily she turned her head, trying to find a more comfortable spot on the pillow.

She was sound asleep half an hour later, when Kyle walked quietly up to the bed. As he looked down at her, his expression was tortured and full of pain. He almost reached out to touch her, but just in time he controlled the impulse.

Ten minutes later he left the house, driving David's Land Rover, heading to the remote farmhouse.

He didn't stay there long; ten minutes was more than enough time for him to vent his wrath on a man who had committed what he considered to be the most despicable crime any man could commit, bar that of damaging a child. He didn't resort to physical violence; he didn't need to.

Curtly ordering David into the passenger seat of the Land Rover, he drove back in silence, stopping it at the end of his own drive and getting out.

'It was her own fault, Bennett,' David whined, moving cautiously into the driver's seat as Kyle stood and watched him. 'She as good as asked for it, telling everyone that she had lived with you. Implying that the two of you had been lovers. Everyone heard her.'

And as he drove away David couldn't understand the brief flash of surprised pleasure that had lightened the dark, bitterly angry features of the man standing watching him. What on earth had he said that had pleased him so much?

He hadn't expected Kyle to come seeking him out. He had judged the other man by his own code of behaviour. He would have to make sure that none of what had happened tonight got back to his cronies' ears. He would be a laughing stock if it did.

Kyle didn't wait to watch him drive away, but walked up the drive. It was cold, the sky clear and brilliant with stars. As he drew in a deep lungful of the crisp air he turned towards the house and wondered exactly why Heather had implied that the two of them had once been lovers. Physically she wanted him, he knew that. But that wasn't enough and it never would be enough. Stretching aching muscles, he walked more slowly toward the house.

CHAPTER NINE

HEATHER woke up with a start. Her mouth was dry, her heart pounding rapidly with fear. She could feel it in the air around the bed, and the shreds of her nightmare still clung to her, bemusing her, even though she realised that there was nothing to fear.

Something moved in the shadows and she screamed involuntarily.

'Heather, what's wrong?'

How had Kyle managed to reach her room so quickly? He must have already been awake.

He looked tired, Heather thought as he snapped on the light, banishing the vague spectres of her fears.

'A bad dream. I'm sorry I woke you.'

She watched as he pushed unsteady fingers through his already tousled hair.

'You didn't,' he told her shortly. 'I was awake already.' He looked away from her and, for the first time since she had known him, Heather saw something approaching vulnerability and uncertainty shadow his face.

'Heather, what you said about still being a virgin . . .'

He hesitated slightly as though searching for the right words, and, already shrinking away from the pity she was sure she was going to see in his eyes, Heather fought to keep it at bay, snapping sharply.

'Are you accusing me of lying? What do you want me to do, Kyle? Prove it to you?'

An awful silence fell. Without any cloaking darkness to hide the brilliant colour scorching her skin, Heather knew that Kyle must be fully aware of her embarrassment. *Why* had she said that? It didn't take the brain of Freud to deduct that there had been more than a touch of wishful thinking, more than just a mere desire to taunt him behind her challenge. She already knew full well that Kyle hadn't been accusing her of lying, or anything like that. He had simply been trying to express his concern for her. He had been trying to play the role of brother, but she had destroyed that carefully erected façade, and with those few impulsive words had laid bare for both of them the reality of the sexual awareness between them.

For one long moment, they looked at one another. Kyle didn't attempt to hide from her how much he wanted her. She felt her heart thud heavily against her breastbone, and her breath quicken with excitement.

'Is that what you want me to do?' he asked her softly at last, and then, when she made no reply, he came closer to the bed, a dark, aroused flush of colour staining the bones of his face.

'Do you *know* the temptation offered to me, I wonder?' he groaned unsteadily. 'Do you know how often I've dreamed of having you in my arms, your body against mine? You can't even begin to imagine what it does to me to know that there's been no other man. *Why*, Heather?' he demanded, his voice suddenly velvet rough with male desire. 'Was it because you've been waiting for *me*? For this?'

She could have stopped him, she ought to have stopped him. She should have told him that he was wrong, that she didn't want him, and that her virginity was a result of chance and nothing else, but she was already in his arms and his mouth was moving on her skin with a hungry urgency that left her no room for thought.

Its slow and deliberate progress across her eyelids and cheekbones was infinite pleasure and infinite torture. She ached for him to kiss her properly, and with a wantonness the old Heather would never have exhibited she reached impatiently towards him, tugging on the thick softness of his hair until he lifted his mouth and she was able to press her lips against his in an aching torment of need.

She just caught his indrawn breath of incredulity, a brief moment of tension before he hesitated and looked down into her eyes, as though searching for something. She froze, not sure why he was hesitating, her old insecurities urging her to retreat. But as though he sensed her withdrawal, Kyle held on to her, bending his head and muttering something incomprehensible against her lips.

He said it again and this time she heard it, her skin crawling with heat and desire as he repeated thickly, 'Open your mouth and kiss me properly. God, Heather, you can't know how I've ached for the taste of you, for the feel of you, wanting me like this.'

Blindly she obeyed his command, aroused by the tone of his voice and its raw undercurrent of sexuality, almost as much as she was by his touch. Her lips parted, and she shivered beneath the rough caress of his tongue. She could feel his heart ham-

mering against her skin, and she moaned protestingly at the restriction of their clothes.

She wanted to feel his body against her own, to
stroke his skin and to know its silken warmth. She
wanted to explore the male body that seemed so
strong and inviolate, and yet that trembled at her
lightest touch.

She felt the impassioned thrust of Kyle's tongue,
and accepted its dominance, letting herself melt into
him, moaning a frustrated protest at the barriers
between them.

'What is it?' Kyle demanded, lifting his mouth
from hers. He was breathing very fast, his skin
flushed and hot. She raised her hand to touch his
face, wondering at its heat and strength, and he
caught her wrist, touching his lips to her fingertips.
Just the sensation of his breath against her skin was
enough to make her quiver with need.

'What's wrong?' he demanded again.

How could she tell him that she ached to feel the
hardness of his body against her? That she longed
for him to remove the mutual barrier of their clothes
and to cover her instead with the hot skin of his
flesh? She couldn't.

'It's the light,' she fibbed huskily instead. 'It's
so bright.'

'If I go and switch if off, will you promise me
that you won't disappear?' he muttered urgently
against her throat. 'I'm so afraid that you're just
a mirage, a figment of my imagination, a Heather
conjured up by my l... need for you.'

Had she imagined that tiny check? What had he
been about to say before he changed his mind? She
shivered as he got up to snap off the light. Before

she had had a chance to accustom herself to the darkness he was back, taking her into his arms, kissing her with a fierce urgency that set her on fire. She trembled and then shivered beneath the intensity of his desire.

'What is it, what's wrong? Are you cold?'

She shivered harder beneath the slurred passion in his voice. The sound of it was like the purr of a wild animal, fascinating and dangerous at the same time.

'You're shivering.' His arms tightened, constricting her breathing.

'Only because I've never...I've never felt like this before.'

The admission was out before caution could silence it. For a moment she thought he was angry, and then he moved and she saw his face in the faint light coming in through the window.

What she saw there made her catch her breath in wonder. She had never imagined that any man could look like that for her.

She reached blindly towards him, and he gathered her against his body, holding her so that she felt every straining muscle; so that she was immediately and shockingly aware of his arousal.

'I didn't know.' She whispered the words more for her own benefit than for his, but he heard them and asked roughly,

'What? That you could make me feel like this, and share that feeling. Is that what you didn't know?' His voice was like a caress, soothing and yet exciting her at the same time. 'Don't ask me to let you go, because I can't. I've wanted you for too long, Heather.'

He picked her up and she knew, before he put her down on the bed, what he was going to do. As he bent over her, she shook her head and he tensed.

'What is it?'

She heard the strain in his voice, and it melted away the last of her doubts. This was no dominating male, confident of his power over her, but another human being, as vulnerable in his desire as she was herself. A man who wanted her and whom, in turn, she wanted. She felt no fear or apprehension, only a marvellous sense of release and rightness.

'The first time your body touches mine, I want it to be without any barriers between us.'

For a moment she thought she had shocked him, and then he moved. Although his hands trembled slightly, he removed both his clothes and her own; there was no hesitation in either his movements or his voice as he gently covered her body with the silken strength of his own and said quietly, 'You mean like this?'

She could hardly speak, she was trembling so much. Nothing had prepared her for the sheer pleasure of being so close to him; the weight of him pressing her down against the mattress, the small movement of his torso as he talked to her causing an almost unbearable frisson of pleasure to pulse through her breasts.

He caught her soft gasp and instantly his eyes locked on her.

'What is it?' he whispered. 'This?'

He moved again, deliberately and erotically, and fierce pangs of desire raced through her.

'You like that?'

She could hear the male satisfaction in his voice, but for once it didn't anger her.

'Yes,' she whispered back. 'Yes, I like it very much.'

She closed her eyes and gave herself up to the voluptuous swell of pleasure surging through her as Kyle bent his head and slowly traced a line of tormenting kisses from the base of her throat to the swell of her breasts.

She didn't need any coaxing or urging to arch up against his mouth when it finally reached the tautness of her nipple. The gentle rhythmic caress of his lips as they tugged softly on the erect nub of flesh brought wave after wave of fierce delight rolling through her body, and yet her senses told her that there was more, that Kyle was deliberately holding back.

When she moaned and pressed his head to her breast, he eased away.

'Heather, no,' he protested. 'This is all very new to you and I don't want . . . I don't want to do anything that might hurt you.'

Once, she would have taken that as a rejection, but now she had enough intuition to sense the frustrated desire behind the denial and, wantonly, she arched up against him, lifting her head so that she could whisper pleadingly, 'I'm a woman and not a child, Kyle, and that's how I want you to make love to me. I can't help it if I haven't experienced any of this before, but . . .'

'You can't *help* it! Do you honestly think I'm objecting?' He groaned. 'Oh, God, Heather!'

Her lungs seized up in a paralysis of pleasure as his mouth held hers, his teeth tugging at her bottom lip, his need of her so obvious and so almost out of control that she couldn't suppress the deep wave of feminine excitement shivering through her.

Voluptuously, she allowed her instinct to take over. When again his lips caressed the sensitive flesh of her nipple, her fingertips stroked the hard ridge of his spine. His gentleness vanished, his mouth fierce in its possession of her breasts, the faint pain of the sharp rasp of his teeth against the sensitive tissue lost beneath the intensity of her pleasure.

Wherever his mouth touched her, her flesh responded, delighting in the sensation. Boldly she caressed him in turn, filled with wonderment that she had gone so long without knowing how much she loved him. Blocking out of her mind the fact that he only desired her, she gave herself to their lovemaking with the passionate intensity of her nature.

Long before the final act of possession she was aching for the pleasure of having Kyle within her. Her femininity clamoured for it, ached for it, demanded it, and when Kyle hesitated, searching her face for signs of reluctance or apprehension, she clung to him.

'Now, Kyle . . . now, please.'

She closed her eyes as she felt his body surge against her own, and then opened them in disappointment and fear as he stopped.

'That's better. I want to look at you as I make love to you. Heather, I want to see what you're feeling reflected in your eyes, and I want you to see what loving you is doing to me.'

In its own way, it was almost more intimate than the physical union of their bodies. In Kyle's eyes she saw the same fierce pleasure she herself was experiencing: the same exultation, the same humbling of pride and self to the demands of their flesh.

She cried out and didn't know that she had done so until she heard Kyle's hoarse response, her body gripped by intense surges of sensation. She felt the heat and power of Kyle's body within her own and welcomed its strength, exulting in her own power at the moment of their mutual release from earthly bonds.

'Yes ... yes ... that's how I wanted to see you,' she heard Kyle say, fiercely. 'Now I know that you're really mine. Nothing could have prevented this from happening, Heather, it was written in our lives too long ago.'

The pleasure was fading, leaving her tremulous and exhausted, and yet exultant at the same time. Willingly, she let Kyle draw her close to him, as he eased her damp, exhausted body close to his own. She could still feel the frantic racing of his heart. She covered it with her palm, smiling to herself to think that she had the power to affect him so strongly.

Her last thought as she fell asleep was that she loved him.

Heather woke up abruptly just before dawn, shivering with cold, and then realised why. Kyle had left her. She shivered again, every slight movement of her body reminding her of the intensity of their lovemaking. Now, alone and completely free of shock and trauma, she was forced to consider the folly of what she had done.

Where would she and Kyle go from here? He had said nothing about loving her; he had made no promises to her. There had been no talk of any future for their relationship.

Her immediate instinct was to leave, to hide herself away somewhere where she could be alone to contemplate her future, but she couldn't do that. This afternoon her parents were expecting her and Kyle to drive them to the airport for their flight to Portugal.

It struck her as she sat there, her coldness forgotten, that Kyle probably felt exactly the same way as she did herself, that there was possibly nothing more he wanted than for her to disappear out of his life. Last night had been an aberration for both of them; a coming together that was a culmination of something begun many years ago. Now it was over; that part of their lives finally finished. She didn't regret their making love. How could she? Even now, the memory of the pleasure he had given her lingered in her body, and she knew shamefully that, if he were to come to her now, physically she would be unable to stop herself from welcoming him.

No, she couldn't do anything until after her parents had left. Her mind raced round in tormented circles. She would have to go home. The house would be cold and unwelcoming, but better that than staying here, embarrassing Kyle with her presence. How long would it be before he put two and two together and guessed the truth? That was a complication that would benefit neither of them. She still retained enough pride to want to meet Kyle on equal terms, but she couldn't. He had never deceived her. He had never said anything about loving her, probably had no idea of how she felt about him, and that was the way she would prefer it to stay.

But what if, last night, she had conceived his child? Her heart skipped a beat, thudding rapidly and unevenly as she dwelt on the prospect with a mingling of dread and desire. What had happened to her, that she should actually be half hoping that she would have his child? To even contemplate the possibility was sheer self-indulgent fantasy.

Incredibly, she fell asleep again, waking only when her alarm went off some hours later.

She told herself that she should be either disappointed or surprised to find that Kyle had left the house. He had left a note for her and she read it slowly.

'Had to go into the office on urgent business. Back in time to take your parents to the airport.'

Had he really had to go out, or was that just a manufactured excuse to spare them both any embarrassment? In all honesty, could she have faced him across the breakfast table this morning without betraying how she felt?

She didn't know, but she did know that she felt bereft and abandoned by his absence.

It was half-way through the morning before she spared David a thought. No doubt he would have found some way of getting himself home. It was odd to think that, if it hadn't been for him, last night might never have happened.

Kyle's cleaner had returned from her sister's and arrived just after eleven. She was a small, thin woman who moved and spoke very quickly. Heather had half expected her to exhibit at least some curiosity concerning her own presence, but

she was very quickly made aware of Mrs Evans'
dislike of 'prying into other folks' business, and
them into mine'.

Taking the hint, Heather left the woman to her
work. Kyle had promised that after they had seen
her parents off he would take her to show her the
new shopping complex. She couldn't work for him
now, of course, he wouldn't want her to, anyway.

The phone rang, and she answered it automatically, tensing when she heard Kyle's voice.

'I was just ringing to let you know that I'm
leaving the office soon. Has Mrs Evans arrived?'

'Yes, she's here.'

How odd that she was able to speak so normally
when her heart was pumping like a steam engine,
and her pulse was racing frantically at the mere
sound of his voice.

'Good. She'll organise something for lunch, so
don't worry about that.'

He hesitated, as though wanting to say something else, but for the life of her Heather couldn't
dredge up the self-confidence to fill the small betraying silence. She heard another telephone ring,
and wondered which of them it was who gave that
faint, relieved sigh as Kyle said quickly, 'I'm sorry,
I have to go, the other phone's ringing. I should be
back for half-past one, tell Mrs Evans.'

It was funny, but for a second or so Heather felt
as though Kyle was searching for some way to re-
assure and comfort her. And yet, why should he
bother to do that? Why should he concern himself
with her feelings at all? And, most of all, why was
it that where she had previously been so blind to
all his good points, she was now so acutely aware

of his concern and compassion, his caring love for her parents, and his desire to protect them from hurt and pain? She was jealous of Kyle's love for her parents. How ridiculous and how pointless. Restlessly she went to find Mrs Evans, so that she could relay Kyle's message to her.

Heather heard the Jaguar the moment it turned into the drive, and only just managed to restrain herself from leaping to her feet and rushing to meet Kyle.

Instead she stayed decorously where she was, not even getting up out of her chair as he walked into the room. He still looked tired, and somehow defeated as well. As he looked at her, just for a moment she sensed an aura of depression and disappointment about him, but, since she evaded looking directly at him for fear of what she might betray, she decided that she must be imagining things.

'Mrs Evans has just left. Lunch is all ready.'

She knew that she was babbling, but she was desperate to fill the constrained silence.

'Heather . . . about last night . . .'

Immediately she panicked, dreading what he might be going to say and forestalling him. 'I don't want to talk about it, please, Kyle. Not before we've seen my parents off. Can't we leave it . . . for now?'

His mouth tightened grimly.

'If that's what you want.' He walked over to her, and stood in front of her so that she was forced to look up at him. 'You can't push it out of sight for ever, though, Heather. Sooner or later, you're going to have to face the fact that . . .'

'That we went to bed together? Kyle, you're making a fuss about nothing...I...I can't talk about it now. Please, let's leave it until after.'

'Very well.' He wasn't pleased, she could tell that. What was he frightened of? That she would try to cling to him? Never!

Neither of them did justice to Mrs Evans' delicious lunch. Heather could only endure sitting there with him by completely putting from her mind the events of the previous night.

They set off for the hospital shortly after two. Kyle drove, and as she sat in silence at his side Heather was acutely aware of him.

It seemed ironic now that she had never realised before what lay at the root of her almost desperate determination to dislike him. Part of her had known even then that this could happen, but had hidden that knowledge from herself.

They reached the hospital in good time. Her father was as excited and happy as a small child. He had always taken such pleasure in so many small aspects of life; pleasure that seemed to pass other people by. When she'd been a child, he had opened her eyes to so much that was denied to others, Heather recognised, smiling back at him. In his smile she read his pleasure at seeing her in apparent accord with Kyle, his excitement at the coming trip, and his relief that his hospital ordeal was over. Her mother stood at his side, less ebullient, more restrained, but just as thrilled, none the less. Heather turned to look at her and just caught the look that she and Kyle exchanged, conspiratorial and protective. Unobtrusively she touched Heather's father's arm, drawing his attention away from the small group of hospital staff wishing him well.

'It's time we left, darling. We don't want to miss the flight.'

The nurse Kyle had hired was meeting them at the airport. Looking at her father, seeing him restored to his old self, Heather acknowledged that, even if she could not have loved Kyle for any other reason, she must have loved him for this. Without his help, his money, this operation would not have been possible, nor this convalescence.

'You're very quiet, darling,' her mother whispered to her when they reached the airport and she was left standing with her parents while Kyle went to sort out their flight details. 'Is . . . is everything all right?'

The anxiety that momentarily shadowed her mother's eyes hurt her. 'Everything's fine.' Heather assured her, tucking her arm through her mother's and smiling as genuinely as she could. 'Kyle and I . . .' she swallowed. 'I've realised what an idiot I was all those years ago,' she admitted quietly. 'I realised it long ago, in fact, but it was too late then, Kyle had already left.'

As though she read the guilt in her eyes, her mother responded lovingly, 'We were as much to blame, if blame is the right word. We should have given more thought to how having another child living with us would affect you, but darling, I promise you we never stopped loving you. You are *our* child . . .'

Now, having made love with Kyle and knowing however remote a possibility it was that she might have conceived his child, Heather knew exactly what her mother meant. No child born out of love such as she bore Kyle, and such as her parents shared, could ever be supplanted by a child not created in that union, no matter how well loved that other child might be. She was special to her parents because she was the product of their enduring love for one another.

'They're all ready for you.'

Kyle was coming back, accompanied by the nurse and a member of the airport staff. Very discreetly her father was helped into a wheelchair and escorted through the airport formalities. They were allowed to accompany him as far as the barrier, where a very efficient steward took over, carrying her mother's hand luggage and smoothing their progress.

Kyle had organised all that. Kyle's love for her parents was such that no expense or consideration was spared in their care and comfort. Stupid tears stung her eyes, and she didn't really know whether they were for herself or for the lonely little boy her parents had fostered all those years ago.

'If you want to watch them take off we'd better make a move.'

Silently Heather followed him, one part of her aching to be free of the torment of his company, the other longing to prolong it. She was a mass of tensions and nerves, longing for him to say something, to break the taut silence, and yet at the same time dreading hearing the words that would confirm what she already knew: that, for him, last night had simply been a pleasant interlude, and that he had no desire for her to attach any emotional importance to it.

They watched in silence as the plane took off, and then once it had disappeared Heather automatically followed Kyle as he turned to leave.

He paused to open a door for her, and as she hesitated to allow someone else to precede her his hand touched the small of her back, urging her forward. Even through her layers of clothes she was immediately aware of his touch. Her whole body burned, the hot flush darkening her face betraying her agitation. She knew that Kyle must be as aware of her reaction as she was herself, but he made no comment. They walked side by side to the car park, and Heather couldn't help wondering what he was thinking. His thoughts were not hers to concern herself with, she told herself sharply. That chapter of her life, short and bitter-sweet though it had been, was over.

CHAPTER TEN

'This isn't the way back to your house.'

They had left the airport behind, and Heather frowned as she recognised the familiar environs of Bath.

'No, I said I'd show you the site of the new shopping arcade. Give you a taste of what your new job will involve.'

She sat back, half shocked, half thrilled. He still intended to give her the job? She was surprised, she couldn't deny it. Unless... her whole body went cold, and she rubbed instinctively at her goose-pimpled arms. Unless it was because of her parents that he still intended to employ her; because he didn't want to hurt or worry them; because he knew how pleased they would be to learn that she had a safe, secure job with him that wouldn't take her too far away from them. But how *could* she accept employment on those terms? She wanted him to want and value her for herself. If he couldn't love her, then surely at least she could have his respect? And taking a job that was purely and simply a sinecure was no way to achieve that. Besides, how could she work for him, feeling as she did? It was impossible.

It was equally impossible for her not to be impressed when Kyle stopped the car a few yards short of the half-restored arcade.

It was very much as he had described to her, and from the section of the arcade which was already partially restored it was possible to see what the finished effect would be. The Georgian bow windows cried out for subtle, delicate decoration, the traditional cobbled pedestrian-way invited people to linger.

There would be benches at intervals, and a traditional form of street lighting. The opportunity to orchestrate a unifying flow of window décor for the entire complex was one that couldn't be turned down lightly. Heather tried not to allow herself to imagine the pleasure she could have found in the work if she and Kyle were meeting as equals. She couldn't do it. She couldn't take a job that was being offered to her simply because of her parents.

'Kyle . . .' She turned to tell him as much but he was frowning, his voice clipped.

'Heather, I *know* what you're thinking. What you're going to say. I can't in all honesty pretend that I can forget last night, but I promise you I won't let it interfere in our business relationship, if that's what's worrying you. You won't have to pay for your job by sleeping with the boss.' He said the words with distaste, his mouth contorted in a faint grimace. 'For your parents' sake, though, if nothing else, I want you to promise me that you won't leave either my home or my employ. Promise me.'

A cold wind whistled through the deserted arcade, making her shiver. 'Promise me.' She was trapped and they both knew it. How quickly he had divined her intentions! But it wasn't as easy as that.

Her breath shook in her lungs as she breathed in. She mustn't let herself be tied to a promise she wasn't sure she could keep.

'Kyle, I don't think I can make that sort of commitment. After last night...well, you must see how difficult it would be.'

He wasn't going to make it any easier for her, she recognised, facing his grim silence.

'For me to work for you would be bad enough, but to carry on living with you...that would be intolerable for both of us. You must see that,' she pleaded wildly.

'As a matter of fact, I don't. What's so different, other than the fact that we've made love? You can't spend the rest of your life running away from situations you can't face up to. I'm sorry if...' He saw her shiver in the cold and broke off. 'This isn't the place to discuss this. Let's go home.'

There was no point in arguing with him now, Heather consoled herself, as she meekly went with him to the car.

She would tell him tonight of her plans to return home. She fell asleep on the way back, waking only when Kyle shook her. When she opened her eyes she couldn't remember where she was. To open her eyes and see Kyle looking down at her made her forget reality in favour of fantasy. Without even thinking what she was doing she reached out to him, checking herself abruptly when the bright arc of another vehicle's headlights cut through the darkness.

The other vehicle stopped, and then a door opened. A man walked round to Kyle's door.

'We've brought the tree you ordered, Mr Bennett. Where would you like it?'

'If you could take it round the back for me, John, that would be fine.'

The look of pain and disappointment she had thought she had seen in his eyes as she withdrew from him must have been nothing more than a product of her own imagination, Heather acknowledged dully as she got out of the car.

'You go in,' Kyle instructed her. 'I'll go with John.'

She paused for a moment, watching him stride away to help the other man manhandle the large Christmas tree tied to the back of the his small van.

She hadn't envisaged Kyle involved in anything as ordinary as putting up a real Christmas tree. She had half expected him to ignore that aspect of the seasonal festivities, and instead perhaps settle for some outrageously expensive and chic minimalistic Christmas décor.

'I thought we'd dress it this evening,' he told her, walking into the sitting-room later to find her standing in front of it.

This was her opportunity to tell him that she wouldn't be there this evening, that she was leaving, returning to her own home; but stupidly she found herself agreeing, knowing even as she did so that the greater part of her wanted to stay. It was no use telling herself that her behaviour was dangerously close to emotional suicide. Dangerous not because she wanted to stay, but because she *wanted* to be with Kyle.

After they had eaten, Kyle went upstairs and returned with several large cardboard boxes.

'I think there should be enough stuff in here. I'll check the lights and you can sort the rest.'

It was such a familiar and comforting ritual, and one she had shared in so many, many times.

She tried not to think about the first Christmas without Kyle. They had all been subdued, even though her parents had pretended not to be. She had looked in vain for a card from him, believing with all the passionate intensity of her eighteen years that her life could only return to normal once she had some sign from him that she was forgiven.

It was only slowly and painfully that she had learned that that sort of forgiveness could not be bestowed by anyone else, but had to come from within oneself.

'You're looking very pensive. What's on your mind?'

Here was her chance to tell him that she must leave, but foolishly she said nothing, denying that there was anything worrying her.

She watched him surreptitiously as he worked. His hands were strong and sure, and yet careful. He had infinite patience, she reflected, watching him. One day he would marry and have children, she was sure of it, and she was pierced by jealousy at the thought.

The tree was large and it took them two hours to dress it to their mutual satisfaction.

'Are you expecting many guests for Christmas?' Heather asked him, as she stepped back to study it from a distance.

'No, there'll just be two of us.'

His reply shocked her, her hand stilling as she reached out to adjust a piece of tinsel.

'Just . . . but . . .'

'You've been through a very traumatic time recently. I didn't think you'd be in the mood for a horde of house guests.'

She blinked, stunned that he should even have considered her feelings. Ridiculously, all she could think of to say was a husky, 'And I haven't even got you a present.'

'You've already given it to me.'

For a moment she couldn't think, much less speak, her breath trapped deep in her lungs, her mind shocked by what she had heard, and then the intimacy of those few quiet words hit her, and with a small cry she rushed past him and up the stairs.

In her bedroom she sank down on to the bed, shivering with a mixture of sensations. Why had he had to say that? She had suspected him of irony or worse, but hadn't been able to see any in his face, and yet he couldn't have meant to imply that . . . he couldn't really have felt that passionate sincerity she had heard in his voice.

'Heather?'

She held her breath as she heard him outside her door.

'I didn't mean to upset you. Please come back down. I've arranged for us to telephone your parents at ten.'

Unwillingly, Heather opened the door. He looked paler than usual and his face seemed thinner. He needed a shave, and she ached to reach out and touch the roughness of his jaw. A faint smile touched her mouth as she looked at him.

'What's wrong?'

'Nothing, I was just admiring your "designer stubble".'

He frowned and she had to explain what she meant.

'It's supposed to be a big turn on,' she added wryly. 'Pop stars deliberately cultivate it, because they think it makes them look sexy.'

'And what do you think?' he asked her softly.

She was treading on dangerous ground, and if she wasn't careful she was going to find herself admitting that, as far as she was concerned, he didn't need any aids to increase his sexuality. Evasively she replied, 'I'm not really into pop stars any more.'

When they got through to her parents, they were just settling down for the evening. Heather spoke to both of them and was delighted to hear her father sounding so well and relaxed.

When she had finished she handed the receiver over to Kyle. While he spoke to them she looked at the Christmas tree. It was going to be an odd sort of Christmas this year. She tried not to feel abandoned because she wouldn't be spending it with her family.

Shortly after Kyle had replaced the receiver she excused herself, fibbing that she was tired and wanted an early night.

Instantly his expression darkened.

'I thought you and I were going to talk,' he said quietly. 'What is it, Heather?' he demanded when she made no response. 'Is the fact that you and I have been lovers really so repulsive to you that you can't even bear to talk about it? What if we have a child? There *is* that possibility, you know. I...I didn't use any...anything, and since you were a virgin I assume that you...'

'Yes...that is, no...I didn't take any precautions.' She knew that her face was hot with embarrassed colour. He was quite right, of course, although she calculated that the chances of her becoming pregnant were very small.

'If you have conceived my child we shall have to get married. No...please, let me finish. You know what my background is, I can well understand how any woman would feel about having a child by a man who knows nothing of his father and whose mother virtually deserted him, but I have to say this. I won't let you have an abortion, and I certainly won't let you bring my child up alone. I have very strong feelings on the subject, I'm sure you'll understand why. We...'

'We can't get married.' Panic drove her voice into a high-pitched protest as she contemplated the sheer anguish of being married to Kyle simply because she was the mother of his child.

'Heather...'

She jumped up, shaking her head. 'No...I don't want to talk about it. We don't know if I could get pregnant yet. Oh, God, I wish...'

'That you'd never met me?' Kyle supplied for her. 'You haven't changed at all really, have you, Heather? You still loathe and resent me as much as you always did.' He got up as well. 'Very well, we won't discuss it tonight. It's been a long day, but I warn you, if you are carrying my child...'

Heather wouldn't let him finish, interrupting wildly, 'That's all that matters to you, isn't it? I'm just totally unimportant...incidental. It doesn't matter what I think or feel.'

'Heather!'

He called her back as she opened the door, but she couldn't listen to any more. Of course, she could understand how he felt, but that didn't ease her pain; that didn't stop her from experiencing the agony of knowing that to him she was just someone he would have to endure for the sake of his child.

She wasn't pregnant, she was sure of it, just as she was equally sure that Kyle wasn't going to let her out of his sight willingly until she managed to convince him that she was right. It wouldn't be easy. She knew that already. If she left now, and returned home as she had planned, he would suspect that she was trying to deceive him. If she stayed...if she stayed, she would be able to convince him eventually that she wasn't having his child, but she would also run the risk of betraying to him how she felt about him.

She was caught in a cleft stick, Heather acknowledged wearily, and faced with a problem to which there appeared to be no straightforward solution.

She was no closer to finding one on Christmas Eve. Mrs Evans had arrived later than usual, complaining that she wasn't feeling well. She hadn't slept for several days, she told Heather, and to make matters worse her husband wasn't well, either.

Heather listened to her with one ear as she helped the other woman prepare for the holiday weekend. How was she going to feel tomorrow, sharing her Christmas lunch with Kyle, being alone with him all day?

This morning he was working. An urgent phone call had taken him into his office. Already, in a frighteningly short time she had allowed him to become too important to her. How was she going to feel when eventually she found the strength to walk away? It wasn't going to be easy. Only she knew how much time she spent fantasising about their one night together, trying to imagine what it would be like to live with him properly and share his life.

She glanced at Mrs Evans. The older woman did look white and tired. On impulse, Heather offered to go upstairs and bring down a couple of Kyle's sleeping tablets.

'I'm sure he won't mind, and they should ensure that you get at least one good night's sleep.'

'Well, if you're sure he won't mind. I don't like bothering the doctor. Not at this time of year. Well, they get so busy, don't they?'

'I'm sure Kyle won't mind at all,' Heather assured her. 'I won't be a minute.'

She brought the whole bottle down. Mrs Evans was ready and waiting to leave, but as Heather uncapped the bottle the phone rang. As she picked it up, the bottle slipped from her fingers, the tablets scattering all over the sitting-room floor.

'Don't worry about them. I'll pick them up later,' she mouthed to Mrs Evans, offering her two from the few that still remained in the bottle.

She took them with a smile and mouthed back, 'I'll let myself out. Have a good Christmas.'

Kyle had already given Mrs Evans her Christmas bonus. Once she had gone, Heather concentrated on listening to her mother, who had rung to tell her how well her father was doing.

'I miss you,' Heather confessed. 'Christmas won't be the same without you.'

A little to her chagrin, her mother made no reply, and said instead, 'How's Kyle? I've been worrying about him. He works far too hard.'

'He's working this morning, but he should be back soon.'

No sooner had she replaced the receiver than the milkman arrived. Kyle had given her an envelope for him which she had left upstairs. As she raced up to get it she heard Kyle's car arrive. While she paid the milkman at the back door, she heard Kyle come in and walk into the sitting-room.

She had just closed the back door when she heard him call her name, and she froze at the sound of harsh anguish that filled the hallway.

Unable to move, she heard him rush upstairs, still calling her name. He sounded like a man demented by the possibility of some unimaginable grief.

Like a sleep-walker, she went into the hall.

'Kyle, I'm here.'

For a moment she thought he hadn't heard her, and then he stopped and turned. 'Oh, my God, are you all right?'

She was standing at the bottom of the stairs when he reached her, and she could feel his whole body shuddering as he wrapped his arms around her.

'Heather, Heather, you little fool. Were you really so desperate to escape from me? How many have you taken?'

She stepped back from him. He shook her violently.

'How many, Heather, damn you? Oh God, I don't know if I can go through this again! Once in one lifetime's enough for any man. Come with me.'

He was dragging her towards the door before she managed to speak.

'Kyle, please stop. I haven't done anything. I'm not trying to escape from you.' She glanced into the sitting-room and saw the spilled tablets. 'Oh, heavens, I forgot about those. I'd better pick them up.'

'You forgot?'

She heard the tormented sound of his voice, and knew then exactly what he had feared. Her own face went almost white as his.

'You thought that I...?' Her eyes rounded with shocked realisation. 'Oh, Kyle, no...Mrs Evans hasn't been sleeping. I gave her two. They spilled out of the bottle. You surely didn't think that I...?'

'Why not?' he accused roughly. 'You did it once before.'

'That was a mistake!' Her anguished cry silenced them both. They faced each other like two adversaries.

'You try to end your own life and almost succeed, and you call that a mistake? For God's sake, Heather, have you any idea how I felt that night when I came back and found you; when I realised that if I hadn't... Have you any idea of what it did to me to know that I was the one who had driven you to that state?' He shook his head, as though trying to ward off bad memories.

'And now I'm doing it again,' he said savagely. 'God, when will I learn that I can't make you love me, that just because you gave yourself to me physically it doesn't mean...' He shook his head again.

'It was because of what I said about the child, wasn't it?' he demanded quietly. 'You couldn't bear the thought of being married to me, of bearing my child, and so instead...'

'I did what, Kyle? Took half a bottle of sleeping tablets?' She shook her head vehemently. 'No way! Do you think I haven't learned from *my* mistakes, too? Do you think I don't have the intelligence to realise how stupid I was? You say you love me.' Her voice shook over the words she had still not fully allowed herself to believe. 'Maybe you do, but you don't seem to know me very well. You're confusing me with a seventeen-year-old spoilt child.'

'What are you trying to tell me?'

He seemed to have recovered some of his familiar self-control; his face was still white and strained, but that blazing look of agony was gone from his eyes.

'I'm trying to tell you that I have too much respect for myself as a person to do anything so foolish.'

'But you hated the thought of being tied to me,' he challenged. 'Don't deny it, I saw it in your eyes.'

'Yes,' she said gravely. 'I hated the thought of being tied to you for the sake of a child I suspect I haven't even conceived.'

He frowned, started to speak and then checked himself. 'What is it you're telling me, Heather?'

'You say you love me. Hasn't it occurred to you that if you'd told me that the night we made love that . . . that it might have made it easier for me to admit my feelings for you, instead of having to try so desperately to conceal them?'

'Your feelings for me?' He seemed almost stupefied. 'But you hate me! That's why I never told you . . .'

'Told me what?' she asked sharply, as he broke off with a muttered curse, dark colour tinging his cheeks.

'That your father's operation could have been performed as an emergency case by the National Health Service. That you could have managed after a fashion without my help. Your mother had begun to make the arrangements before I came on the scene, but she agreed to let me . . . take over. I wanted to do more than pay for the operation, you see; I wanted to give your parents the security they once gave me. And, incidentally, to have an excellent reason to see you every day. And it didn't work, did it? I compromised with my conscience to make you grateful to me, but nothing could change the fact that you hate me.'

'Do I?' she said wryly. 'Is that why I go up in flames every time you come anywhere near me? Is that why I've never wanted any other man to make love to me? Is that why I almost wish I was having your child? Oh, Kyle,' she protested, torn between tears and laughter as he grabbed hold of her, running his hands over her body as though he couldn't believe she was real.

'Six years,' he breathed shakily at last. 'For six years I've dreamed of hearing you say something like this, and now that you are I don't think I can believe it. I thought you hated me.'

'So did I until quite recently, but I knew even before we made love that I was wrong. Kyle!'

'Don't talk,' he muttered thickly against her mouth. 'Kiss me instead.'

It was a long time before he released her.

'I would have helped your parents anyway, you know,' he told her rawly, still holding on to her. 'I love them, Heather, but I kept away for...'

'For my sake...yes, I know,' she agreed quietly. 'It hurt me very badly to have to admit that to myself, Kyle, and to have to admit that it was because of me that my parents deprived themselves of sharing their lives with you.'

'I don't want to talk about the past. Let's talk about the future. *Our* future. You will marry me?'

'If that's what you want.'

'What I want right now,' he groaned, 'is to pick you up, and lie you down right here in front of the fire, and make love to you until you can't think of anything or anyone but me. Twice now I've thought I've lost you, Heather,' he told her huskily. 'There isn't going to be a third time. I'm never going to let you go, so don't ask me to. So tell me now if you don't want me.'

Wrapping her arms around him, and pressing her mouth against his, her body moulding itself to his in an eager caress, she teased against his lips, 'I don't want you.'

But he couldn't have heard her, because he was already picking her up, and she could feel her blood heating in excited anticipation of the pleasure to come. The tablets, still scattered on the floor, were forgotten. The firelight warmed the pale silkiness of her skin and darkened the tanned hardness of Kyle's body. He made love to her with urgency and compulsion, drowning them both in a tidal wave of ecstasy. She slept in his arms and woke to find herself alone. He had tucked his robe around her and propped up beside her a large white envelope with her name on it.

She was just reading the contents when he walked in, wearing another robe and carrying a bottle of champagne and two glasses.

'Your Christmas present,' he told her, getting down beside her as she stared at the two plane tickets inside the Christmas card.

'Did you really think I wouldn't know how much you'd want to spend this Christmas with your parents? I was going to give it to you in the morning. A special Christmas morning surprise, but this way I don't have to wait until tomorrow to see the pleasure in your eyes.' He poured two glasses of champagne and handed her one.

'To us and the future,' he toasted, and as Heather sipped the dancing bubbles happiness fizzed up inside her.

'Make love to me again, Kyle,' she whispered, leaning towards him. 'Make love to me so that I can believe all this is real.'

Later, when their son asked why he was called Noel when he was born in September, she would smile at Kyle and he would smile back at her, both of them knowing that the other was remembering the Christmas Eve they had consummated their love and, or so Heather suspected, she had conceived their first child.

In December,
let Harlequin warm your heart with the
AWARD OF EXCELLENCE title

Harlequin Presents...

PENNY JORDAN

a rekindled passion

Over twenty years ago, Kate had a holiday
affair with Joss Bennett and found herself
pregnant as a result. Believing that Joss had
abandoned her to return to his wife and child,
Kate had her daughter and made no attempt
to track Joss down.

At her daughter's wedding, Kate suddenly
confronts the past in the shape of the
bridegroom's distant relative—Joss. He quickly
realises that Sophy must be his daughter and
wonders why Kate never contacted him.

Can love be rekindled after twenty years?
Be sure not to miss this AWARD OF EXCELLENCE
title, available wherever Harlequin books
are sold.

HP-KIND-1

H·I·S·T·O·R·I·C·A·L
Christmas
S·T·O·R·I·E·S 1·9·9·0

Once again Harlequin, the experts in romance, bring you the magic of Christmas —as celebrated in America's past.

These enchanting love stories celebrate Christmas made extra-special by the wonder of people in love....

Nora Roberts **In From the Cold**
Patricia Potter **Miracle of the Heart**
Ruth Langan **Christmas at Bitter Creek**

Look for this Christmas collection now wherever Harlequin® books are sold.

"Makes a great stocking stuffer."

HX90-1A

Take 4 bestselling love stories FREE

Plus get a FREE surprise gift!

Special Limited-time Offer

Harlequin Reader Service®

Mail to
In the U.S.
3010 Walden Avenue
P.O. Box 1867
Buffalo, N.Y. 14269-1867

In Canada
P.O. Box 609
Fort Erie, Ontario
L2A 5X3

YES! Please send me 4 free Harlequin Presents® novels and my free surprise gift. Then send me 6 brand-new novels every month, which I will receive months before they appear in bookstores. Bill me at the low price of $2.24* each—a savings of 26¢ apiece off cover prices. There are no shipping, handling or other hidden costs. I understand that accepting the books and gift places me under no obligation ever to buy any books. I can always return a shipment and cancel at any time. Even if I never buy another book from Harlequin, the 4 free books and the surprise gift are mine to keep forever.

*Offer slightly different in Canada—$2.24 per book plus 69¢ per shipment for delivery. Sales tax applicable in N.Y.

306 BPA U103 (CAN)

106 BPA CAP7 (US)

Name _____ (PLEASE PRINT)

Address _____ Apt. No. _____

City _____ State/Prov. _____ Zip/Postal Code _____

This offer is limited to one order per household and not valid to present Harlequin Presents® subscribers. Terms and prices are subject to change.

© 1990 Harlequin Enterprises Limited

PASSPORT TO ROMANCE
SWEEPSTAKES RULES

1. **HOW TO ENTER:** To enter, you must be the age of majority and complete the official entry form, or print your name, address, telephone number and age on a plain piece of paper and mail to: Passport to Romance, P.O. Box 9056, Buffalo, NY 14269-9056. No mechanically reproduced entries accepted.

2. All entries must be received by the CONTEST CLOSING DATE, DECEMBER 31, 1990 TO BE ELIGIBLE.

3. **THE PRIZES:** There will be ten (10) Grand Prizes awarded, each consisting of a choice of a trip for two people from the following list:
   i) London, England (approximate retail value $5,050 U.S.)
   ii) England, Wales and Scotland (approximate retail value $6,400 U.S.)
   iii) Carribean Cruise (approximate retail value $7,300 U.S.)
   iv) Hawaii (approximate retail value $9,550 U.S.)
   v) Greek Island Cruise in the Mediterranean (approximate retail value $12,250 U.S.)
   vi) France (approximate retail value $7,300 U.S.)

4. Any winner may choose to receive any trip or a cash alternative prize of $5,000.00 U.S. in lieu of the trip.

5. **GENERAL RULES:** Odds of winning depend on number of entries received.

6. A random draw will be made by Nielsen Promotion Services, an independent judging organization, on January 29, 1991, in Buffalo, NY, at 11:30 a.m. from all eligible entries received on or before the Contest Closing Date.

7. Any Canadian entrants who are selected must correctly answer a time-limited, mathematical skill-testing question in order to win.

8. Full contest rules may be obtained by sending a stamped, self-addressed envelope to: "Passport to Romance Rules Request", P.O. Box 9998, Saint John, New Brunswick, Canada E2L 4N4.

9. Quebec residents may submit any litigation respecting the conduct and awarding of a prize in this contest to the Régie des loteries et courses du Québec.

10. Payment of taxes other than air and hotel taxes is the sole responsibility of the winner.

11. Void where prohibited by law.

COUPON BOOKLET OFFER TERMS

To receive your Free travel-savings coupon booklets, complete the mail-in Offer Certificate on the preceeding page, including the necessary number of proofs-of-purchase, and mail to: Passport to Romance, P.O. Box 9057, Buffalo, NY 14269-9057. The coupon booklets include savings on travel-related products such as car rentals, hotels, cruises, flowers and restaurants. Some restrictions apply. The offer is available in the United States and Canada. Requests must be postmarked by January 25, 1991. Only proofs-of-purchase from specially marked "Passport to Romance" Harlequin® or Silhouette® books will be accepted. The offer certificate must accompany your request and may not be reproduced in any manner. Offer void where prohibited or restricted by law. LIMIT FOUR COUPON BOOKLETS PER NAME, FAMILY, GROUP, ORGANIZATION OR ADDRESS. Please allow up to 8 weeks after receipt of order for shipment. Enter quickly as quantities are limited. Unfulfilled mail-in offer requests will receive free Harlequin® or Silhouette® books (not previously available in retail stores), in quantities equal to the number of proofs-of-purchase required for Levels One to Four, as applicable.

OFFICIAL SWEEPSTAKES ENTRY FORM

Complete and return this Entry Form immediately—the more Entry Forms you submit, the better your chances of winning!
- Entry Forms must be received by **December 31, 1990**
- A random draw will take place on **January 29, 1991**
- Trip must be taken by **December 31, 1991**

3-HP-3-SW

YES, I want to win a PASSPORT TO ROMANCE vacation for two! I understand the prize includes round-trip air fare, accommodation and a daily spending allowance.

Name_____

Address_____

City_____ State_____ Zip_____

Telephone Number_____ Age_____

Return entries to: **PASSPORT TO ROMANCE**, P.O. Box 9056, Buffalo, NY 14269-9056

© 1990 Harlequin Enterprises Limited

COUPON BOOKLET/OFFER CERTIFICATE

Item	LEVEL ONE Booklet 1	LEVEL TWO Booklet 1 & 2	LEVEL THREE Booklet 1, 2, 3	LEVEL FOUR Booklet 1, 2, 3 & 4
Booklet 1 = $100+	$100+	$100+	$100+	$100+
Booklet 2 = $200+		$200+	$200+	$200+
Booklet 3 = $300+			$300+	$300+
Booklet 4 = $400+	_____	_____	_____	$400+
Approximate Total Value of Savings	$100+	$300+	$600+	$1,000+
# of Proofs of Purchase Required	4	6	12	18
Check One	_____	_____	_____	_____

Name_____

Address_____

City_____ State_____ Zip_____

Return Offer Certificates to **PASSPORT TO ROMANCE**, P O Box 9057 Buffalo NY 14269-9057

Requests must be postmarked by **January 25, 1991**

✂- -

ONE PROOF OF PURCHASE

3-HP-3

To collect your free coupon booklet you must include the necessary number of proofs-of-purchase with a properly completed Offer Certificate

© 1990 Harlequin Enterprises Limited

See previous page for details